新·编·大·学·英·语·教·学·配·套·丛·书

大学英语 分级教学同步训练

新题型 **3** 级

College English Practice Tests

Band 3

U0140917

总 主 编 李予军
本册主编 王新刚
副 主 编 杜 曼

国防工业出版社
National Defense Industry Press

内 容 简 介

本书是《新编大学英语教学配套丛书》的第 3 册,内容基本控制在大学英语三级水平要求之内;在题型编排设计上既考虑学生学习现状,又兼顾大学英语四级考试的试题形式,使学生能把学习内容和测试形式结合起来,有针对性地达到训练的目的。全书包括训练试题 10 套,内容涵盖写作、听力理解和听力填空、阅读词汇理解、篇章阅读、阅读简答、词汇和翻译等。书后附有参考答案和听力部分的录音原文。

本书可供大学基础阶段二年级的学生或相当于三级水平的英语学习爱好者使用。

图书在版编目(CIP)数据

大学英语分级教学同步训练新题型 3 级/王新刚
主编.—北京:国防工业出版社,2008.9
(新编大学英语教学配套丛书)
ISBN 978-7-118-05932-8

Ⅰ.大… Ⅱ.王… Ⅲ.英语 – 高等学校 – 习题
Ⅳ.H319.6

中国版本图书馆 CIP 数据核字(2008)第 135132 号

※

国防工业出版社 出版发行

(北京市海淀区紫竹院南路 23 号 邮政编码 100044)
天利华印刷装订有限公司印刷
新华书店经售

*

开本 787×1092 1/16 印张 12¾ 字数 246 千字
2008 年 9 月第 1 版第 1 次印刷 印数 1—5000 册 定价 25.00 元(含光盘)

(本书如有印装错误,我社负责调换)

国防书店:(010)68428422 发行邮购:(010)68414474
发行传真:(010)68411535 发行业务:(010)68472764

《新编大学英语教学配套丛书》
编 写 委 员 会

前　言

　　大学英语教学改革是教育部"高等学校教学改革与教学质量工程"的重要组成部分。《新编大学英语教学配套丛书》正是根据教育部颁发的《大学英语课程教学要求》（以下简称《课程要求》）和《大学英语四、六级考试改革方案（试行）》的精神，结合高校一线教师在大学英语一级至四级的教学和研究中所积累的经验和资料，针对学生在学习、考试中反映出来的问题编写而成的，是探索大学英语教学改革，改进教学模式和教学方法，提高教学效果的一次新尝试。

　　大学英语的教学目的是培养学生的英语综合应用能力。《课程要求》提出各校应根据实际情况制定科学、系统、个性化的大学英语教学大纲，指导本校的大学英语教学。大学阶段英语教学的一般要求是高等学校非英语专业本科毕业生应达到的基本要求。较高要求或更高要求是为有条件的学校根据自己的办学定位、类型和人才培养目标所选择的标准而推荐的。各高等学校应根据本校实际情况确定教学目标并创造条件，使那些英语起点水平较高、学有余力的学生能够达到较高要求或更高要求。这是本丛书编写的理论依据。

　　近年来，一大批专科院校纷纷"升本"。这些院校基本都定位于"应用型"大学，即把培养应用型人才作为自己的培养目标；同时，这些院校还有一个共同的特点，就是生源基本来自"三本"学生。这两个实际情况就决定了这些院校的大学英语教学必须走自己的特色之路，既要努力达到一般要求的规定，又要保证满足一些水平较好的学生的求知欲望。这是本丛书编写的现实依据。

　　《课程要求》指出，教学评估是大学英语课程教学的一个重要环节。全面、客观、科学、准确的评估体系对于实现教学目标至关重要。过去过于关注期中和期末考试，并一度出现"以考代学，以考代教"的现象，导致教学效果不佳，甚至停滞不前。形成性评估是教学过程中进行的过程性和发展性评估，即根据教学目标采用多种评估手段和形式，跟踪教学过程，反馈教学信息，促进学生全面发展。这是本丛书编写的基本指导思想。

　　本丛书主要是配合大学英语教学之用，分为新题型1级、2级、3级、4级和4级冲刺，共5册，分别供大学基础阶段二学年4个学期使用，一学期一级，与教材和教学同步配套使用。每册由3个部分组成：(1)完整的标准模拟试题10套；(2)参考答案和听力原文;(3)配套光盘一张。

本丛书有以下几个主要特点:

1. 严格按照《课程要求》规定和《大学英语四、六级考试改革方案(试行)》的要求,力求体现科学性、实用性和针对性,总结实际教学过程中的经验,结合学生学习的现状,按照标准化的四级考试新题型编写而成,力争突出教材中的重点和难点,旨在通过这些综合内容测试训练,考察学生在综合知识和能力上的掌握程度,并以此作为形成性评估的重要依据和手段。

2. 严格按照《课程要求》精神和规定,突出分级分层教学理念。丛书各分册的内容都分别精选或参考各高校目前的主打教材,紧扣教学内容和教学进度,力求把每册各单元的课程目标和课文重点、难点融入综合测试当中,特别是学生感到难以突破的词汇、完型、翻译和写作;注重学生综合能力和应用能力的培养,既能促进学生有效地掌握语言相关知识和基本技能,又能培养学生自觉的学习意识,开发自主性学习方法。

3. 本丛书各分册试题都是经过精心挑选配套完成的,试题之间、每册之间都有侧重并在难易程度上有区别,特别是在听力、写作题目和要求上更是如此。这既有助于学生在学习过程中注意由易到难的循序过程,也便于教师在教学中不断掌握学生的学习动态,及时调整教学进度和内容。

4. 本丛书既可以作为大学英语教学同步配套教材,也可以用于学生自学自测;既可以整套使用,也可以按需分开使用,以适用于不同阶段不同程度的学生,真正体现出分层、分级、同步和实用,达到训练的目的。另外,本丛书也可供大学基础阶段准备参加各级各类英语考试的学生使用。

参加本丛书编写的人员都是来自首都高校教学第一线的骨干教师,年富力强,具有丰富的教学经验,在编写丛书的同时,也融入了他们自己的教学理念。

在编写过程中,我们参考了部分教科书、参考书和网站的内容,在此特向有关作者、出版单位和网站表示诚挚的谢意。

由于时间仓促,书中难免会有不足之处,恳请广大读者提出宝贵意见和建议。本丛书在编写过程中得到有关方面的大力支持,在此表示衷心的感谢。

编 者

Contents

Model Test 1

Part One Writing

Directions: *For this part, you are allowed 30 minutes to write a composition on the topic given in English. You should write at least 100 words.*

Car Explosion in Beijing

Nowadays, people prefer driving their own cars to taking buses or subways in the big cities, especially in Beijing. While the traffic jams become a headache for the city dwellers. Write an essay commenting on:

1. 现在在大城市,尤其是在北京,人们大都开自己的车,不愿意乘坐公共交通;

2. 大城市私家车剧增的原因;

3. 这种问题可能造成的影响和解决方案。

Part Two Listening Comprehension

Section A

Directions: *In this section you will hear 10 short conversations. At the end of each conversation, a question will be asked about what was said, both the conversation and the question will be spoken only once. After each question there will be a pause. During the pause, you must read the four choices marked A, B, C and D, and decide which is the best answer. Then mark the corresponding letter on the Answer Sheet with a single line through the center.*

1. A. In the supermarket.
   C. Next to the supermarket.
   B. Beside the street.
   D. In the market.

2. A. To see a doctor.
   C. To have a rest.
   B. To go to school.
   D. To have a lunch.

3. A. Go to work.
   C. Go the bank.
   B. Go to the post office.
   D. Go to the airport.

4. A. At home.   B. In a supermarket.

    C. In the restaurant.   D. In the department store.

5. A. Buy a new computer.   B. Do nothing.

    C. Replace a new computer.   D. Repair her computer.

6. A. A hotel clerk and a guest.

    B. A waiter and a customer.

    C. Husband and wife.

    D. A doctor and a patient.

7. A. Eating the seafood.

    B. Visiting some places.

    C. Being tired of the trip.

    D. Her trip to Australia.

8. A. 30 Pounds.   B. 60 Pounds.

    C. 15 Pounds.   D. 13 Pounds.

9. A. 15 minutes.   B. 10 minutes.

    C. 5 minutes.   D. 20 minutes.

10. A. A doctor and a patient.

     B. A salesgirl and a customer.

     C. A waiter and a guest.

     D. Two friends.

Section B

Directions: *In this section, you will hear three short passages. At the end of each passage, you will hear some questions. Both the passage and the questions will be spoken only once. After you hear a question, you must choose the best answer from the four choices marked A, B, C and D, and decide which is the best answer. Then mark the corresponding letter on the Answer Sheet with a single line through the center.*

Passage One

11. A. Over 12.   B. Over 11.   C. Over 13.   D. Over 10.

12. A. Mathematics.   B. Latin.

     C. Geography.   D. French.

13. A. Become old-fashioned.   B. Gain great popularity.
    C. Become well-known.   D. Have a bright future.

Passage Two

14. A. In 1918.   B. In 1907.
    C. In 1908.   D. In 1910.
15. A. In New York   B. In Los Angeles
    C. In Seoul.   D. In Atlanta.
16. A. In 2002   B. In 2000.
    C. In 2003.   D. In 2001.

Passage Three

17. A. On the fourth Thursday in December.
    B. On the fourth Thursday in November.
    C. On the third Thursday in December.
    D. On the fourth Tuesday in November.
18. A. In the 17th century.
    B. In the 16th century.
    C. In the 18th century.
    D. In the 15th century.
19. A. Australia.   B. Africa.
    C. Europe.   D. America.
20. A. God.   B. Their parents.
    C. Indians.   D. Americans.

Section C

Directions: *In this section, you will hear a passage of about 100 words three times. The passage is printed on your Answer Sheet with about 20 words missing. First you will hear the whole passage from the beginning to the end just to get a general idea of it. Then, in the second reading, you will hear a signal indicating the beginning of a pause after each sentence, sometimes two sentences or just part of a sentence. During the pause, you must write down the missing words you have just heard in the corresponding space on the Answer*

3

Sheet. There is also a different signal indicating the end of the pause. When you hear this signal, you must get ready for what comes next from the recording. You can check what you have written when the passage is read to you once again without the pauses.

The history of the English language is ___(21)___ into three periods: The period from ___(22)___ to 1150 is known as the Old English. Old English ___(23)___ differs ___(24)___ ___(25)___ English grammar in these aspects.

The ___(26)___ from 1150 is ___(27)___ as the Middle English period. This period was marked by important ___(28)___ in the English language. The change of this period had a great ___(29)___ on both grammar and ___(30)___. In the meantime many ___(31)___ English words were ___(32)___, but ___(33)___ of words ___(34)___ from French and Latin appeared in the English vocabulary.

Modern English period extends from ___(35)___ to the present day. The Early modern English period extends from 1500 to ___(36)___. The ___(37)___ and ___(38)___ centuries are a period of ___(39)___ expansion for the English vocabulary in the ___(40)___ of the English language.

Part Three   Reading Comprehension

Section A

Directions: *In this section, there is a passage with 10 blanks. You are required to select one word for each blank from a list of choices given in a word bank following the passage. Read the passage through carefully before making your choices. Each choice in the bank is identified by a letter. Please mark the corresponding letter for each item on Answer Sheet with a single line through the center.* **You may not use any of words in the bank more than once.**

Word Bank

A. second	C. which	E. order	G. western	I. with
B. however	D. given	F. Married	H. called	J. first

Chinese family names or surname came into being some 5,000 years ago. There are more than 700 family names in China, of ___(41)___ 20 are common.

In China, the family name precedes the ___(42)___ name, which is occasionally followed by the ___(43)___ name or the western equivalent of a ___(44)___ name. For example, Huang Ming would be ___(45)___ Mr. Huang, and Ming would be his given name. ___(46)___, some Chinese will switch the ___(47)___ of their names when they are dealing ___(48)___ foreigners. Further, many Chinese adopt given names, many of which are ___(49)___ names. ___(50)___ women rarely take their husband's family name in China.

Section B

Directions: *There are 2 passages in this section. Each passage is followed by some questions or unfinished statements. For each of them there are four choices marked A, B, C and D. You should decide on the best choice and mark the corresponding letter on Answer Sheet with a single line through the center.*

Passage One

On December 11, 2001, China officially became the 143rd member of the World Trade Organization (WTO) in the culmination of a negotiation process which began in 1986. Economists have long been debating the global effects of China's accession to the WTO, and as China becomes fully integrated into the organization over the next several years, the accuracy of their predictions will be tested.

One of the biggest residual effects (剩余效应) of China's entry to the WTO, according to economists, will be the relocation of manufacturing and distribution centers to China. Due to its cheap labor, cheap industrial land, and educated workforce, China is an ideal production centre for businesses based in outside countries. This will likely result in a twofold impact — more jobs will be available in China, while countries like India, which have historically offered cheap labor, will suffer. While foreign investment soars in China, other Asian countries suffer. In addition, Mexico and the Caribbean will lose thousands of garment manufacturing jobs as the U.S. lifts restraints on Chinese textile imports.

While the impact on Southeast Asia may be negative, the Western world may benefit. While some suggest China's open borders will result in increased competition and a decreased employment rate for the Western world, Western countries will benefit from access to China's highly developed electronics and industry sectors. With duties and quotas slashed(大量削减), and restrictions lifted, multinationals will benefit by setting up distribution centers without the need for Chinese middlemen.

In conclusion, it seems that while Western countries may benefit from China's accession to the WTO, there's the potential that Asian and South American countries may feel the pinch of free trade as China moves to a global economy.

Questions 51 to 55 are based on the passage.

51. How many members are there in WTO by December, 2001?

    A. 142.   B. 143.   C. 144.   D. 145.

52. How many years did China spend in applying for entry into WTO?

    A. 23.   B. 24.   C. 25.   D. 26.

53. According to the author, which is NOT the reason why China becomes an ideal production centre for businesses?

    A. Open-up and reform policy.

    B. The labor is cheap.

    C. Workforce is educated.

    D. Land used as industries is not expensive.

54. Where did China's entry into WTO have a negative effect on?

    A. Western countries.   B. U.S.A.

    C. East Asia.   D. Southeast Asia.

55. What is the main idea of this article?

    A. History of China's entry into WTO.

    B. The effect of China's entry into WTO.

    C. Role played by China in WTO.

    D. Benefit of Western countries from China's accession to WTO.

Passage Two

William (Bill) H. Gates is chairman of Microsoft Corporation, the worldwide leader in software, services. Born on Oct. 28, 1955, Gates grew up in Seattle with his two sisters. Their father, William H. Gates II, is a Seattle attorney. Their late mother, Mary Gates, was a schoolteacher, University of Washington regent (董事), and chairwoman of United Way International.

Gates attended public elementary school and the private Lakeside School. There, he discovered his interest in software and began programming computers at age 13.

In 1973, Gates entered Harvard University as a freshman. Here, Gates developed a version of the programming language BASIC for the first microcomputer — the MITS Altair.

In his junior year, Gates left Harvard to devote his energies to Microsoft, a company he had begun in 1975 with his childhood friend Paul Allen. Guided by a belief that the computer would be a valuable tool on every office desktop and in every home, they began developing software for personal computers.

Under Gates' leadership, Microsoft's mission has been to continually advance and improve software technology, and to make it easier, more cost-effective and more enjoyable for people to use computers.

In 1999, Gates wrote *Business @ the Speed of Thought*, a book that shows how computer technology can solve business problems in fundamentally new ways. The book was published in 25 languages and is available in more than 60 countries.

Gates was married on Jan. 1, 1994, to Melinda French Gates. They have three children. Gates is an avid reader, and enjoys playing golf and bridge.

Questions 56 to 60 are based on the passage.

56. Where did Bill Gates grow up?

    A. In Seattle.   B. In New York.

    C. In Washington D.C.   D. In Los Angeles.

57. How old did Bill Gates begin programming computers?

    A. 11.   B. 12.   C. 13.   D. 14.

58. How long did Bill Gates stay in Harvard University?

    A. About 1 year.   B. About 2 years.

    C. About 3 years.   D. About 4 years.

59. When was Microsoft established?

    A. In 1972.   B. In 1973.

    C. In 1974.   D. In 1975.

60. What is the main idea of this article?

    A. Brief introduction of Bill Gates.

    B. How Bill Gates set up Microsoft Corporation.

    C. Reasons why Bill Gates established Microsoft Corporation.

    D. Development of Microsoft Corporation.

Part Four   Vocabulary

Directions: *For this part you are required to choose the best answer from A , B , C and D to complete the following sentences.*

61. This is the fourth _____ with law in this year.

    A. brush   B. clash   C. mistake   D. conflict

62. The driver's carefulness led _____ this accident.

    A. with   B. to   C. from   D. in

63. I want to find a job to _____ some money to go traveling aboard.

    A. save for   B. save out   C. save at   D. save up

64. The thief was arrested and _____ to court by the policemen.

    A. take   B. taken   C. bring   D. brought

65. Digital camera is regarded _____ one of the greatest inventions in this century.

    A. as   B. on   C. in   D. with

66. He is quite _____ with the story of Mickey Mouse.

    A. understanding   B. clear

    C. familiar   D. known

67. Mike was praised for succeeding in _____ this question.

    A. answering   B. answer

    C. to answer   D. answered

68. The petty thefts are afraid of the policemen _____ uniform.

    A. on   B. at   C. in   D. with

69. _____ makes it difficult is the complex process.

    A. Which   B. How   C. What   D. Why

70. College students try to find some _____ jobs during their spare times.

    A. temporary   B. permanent   C. full   D. part

71. His success is _____ to his hard work for so many years.

    A. because   B. due   C. owe   D. owning

72. The man is on _____ in the court.

    A. test   B. inspection   C. trial   D. inquiry

73. The accident _____ that he was wrong.

    A. turned up   B. turned on

    C. turned off   D. turned out

8

74. The criminals are those who turn _____ the society.

    A. against   B. out   C. at   D. to

75. I have come to apologize _____ you for bringing you so much trouble.

    A. at   B. to   C. in   D. with

76. He was put into prison because he was _____ of a crime.

    A. guilt   B. guilty

    C. innocent   D. innocence

77. The revolution leaders _____ the farmers to fight for their freedom.

    A. call for   B. call off

    C. call on   D. call in

78. _____ that he was so young, he had done a great job.

    A. Given   B. Give   C. Being given   D. Giving

79. We might _____ a chance of winning if we continue to play as well as we did to-day.

    A. take   B. stand   C. make   D. pick

80. I have no money at present, I have no choice but to _____ my time to pay the debt.

    A. take   B. have   C. spend   D. cost

Part Five   Short Answer Questions

Directions: *In this part there is a short passage with five questions or incomplete statements. Read the passage carefully. Then answer the questions or complete the statement in the fewest possible words.*

    The International Committee of Red Cross (ICRC) is an international organization that cares for the wounded, sick, and homeless in wartime, according to the terms of the Geneva Convention of 1864. It was established in 1863 and was based on the idea of a Swiss businessman called Henry Durant.

    The International Red Cross and Red Crescent Movement refers to all the national and international organizations allowed to use the Red Cross or Red Crescent emblem (标志) and all the activities they undertake to relieve human suffering throughout the world. The International Red Cross and the Red Crescent Movement is one of the largest humanitarian networks in the world with a presence and activities in almost every country. It is unified and guided by seven Fundamental Principles: humanity, impartiality, neutrality, independence, voluntary service, unity and universality. All Red Cross and Red Crescent activities have one central purpose: to help those who suffer, without discrimination whether it be during conflict, in response to natural or man-made disasters, or to alleviate the suffering brought by conditions of chronic poverty.

The International Committee of the Red Cross, the International Federation of Red Cross and Red Crescent Societies and the national societies are independent organizations. Each has its own individual status and exercises no authority over the others.

81. The International Committee of Red Cross was founded in _____.

82. What are the two emblems of the International Red Cross and Red Crescent Movement? _____, _____.

83. Please name seven principles that guide the ICRC.

84. To sum up the purpose of ICRC in your own words.

85. What is the relationship between ICRC and national societies?

Part Six   Translation

Directions: *Finish the sentences on Answer Sheet by translating into English*.

86. 尤其令人烦恼的是,我被捕以及随后在法庭上受审期间所出现的种种武断行为。(arbitrary)

87. 现在,取得驾驶执照的程序变得越来越复杂。(process)

88. 这些天我不得不赚更多的钱,因为下个月租金又要到期了。(due)

89. 大学生们发现毕业后很难找到一份工作。(employment)

90. 人们总是拿他那很重的南方口音开玩笑。(accent)

91. 目击证人将事故那天受害者发生的一切告诉了法官。(witness)

92. 昨天他的所作所为使我更坚信他是一个可靠的人。(confirm)

93. 在会上,人们围绕如何打击恐怖袭击这一话题展开了讨论。(revolve)

94. 大家都不喜欢玛丽,因为她总是怨天尤人。(complain)

95. 他因犯了一个错误受到了惩罚。(commit)

Answer Sheet 1

Part One   Writing

_____
_____
_____
_____
_____
_____
_____
_____
_____
_____
_____
_____
_____
_____
_____
_____
_____
_____
_____
_____
_____
_____
_____
_____
_____

Part Two   Listening Comprehension

Section C

The history of the English language is ___(21)___ into three periods: The period from ___(22)___ to 1150 is known as the Old English. Old English ___(23)___ differs ___(24)___ ___(25)___ English grammar in these aspects.

The ___(26)___ from 1150 is ___(27)___ as the Middle English period. This period was marked by important ___(28)___ in the English language. The change of this period had a great ___(29)___ on both grammar and ___(30)___ . In this period many ___(31)___ English words were ___(32)___ , but ___(33)___ of words ___(34)___ from French and Latin appeared in the English vocabulary.

Modern English period extends from ___(35)___ to the present day. The Early modern English period extends from 1500 to ___(36)___ . The ___(37)___ and ___(38)___ centuries are a period of ___(39)___ expansion for the English vocabulary in the ___(40)___ of the English language.

Part Five   Short Answer Questions

81. _____

_____

82. _____

_____

83. _____

_____

84. _____

_____

85. _____

_____

Part Six   Translation

86. _____

_____

_____

87. _____
    _____
    _____

88. _____
    _____
    _____

89. _____
    _____
    _____

90. _____
    _____
    _____

91. _____
    _____
    _____

92. _____
    _____
    _____

93. _____
    _____
    _____

94. _____
    _____
    _____

95. _____
    _____
    _____

Answer Sheet 2

Part Two   Listening Comprehension
Section A

1	2	3	4	5	6	7	8	9	10

Section B

11	12	13	14	15	16	17	18	19	20

Part Three   Reading Comprehension
Section A

41	42	43	44	45	46	47	48	49	50

Section B

51	52	53	54	55	56	57	58	59	60

Part Four   Vocabulary

61	62	63	64	65	66	67	68	69	70
71	72	73	74	75	76	77	78	79	80

Model Test 2

Part One Writing

Directions: *For this part, you are allowed 30 minutes to write a composition on the topic given in English. You should write at least 100 words.*

The Best Way to Keep Fit

1. 近年来,越来越多的人关注健康问题,关注保持健康的方式;

2. 出现这种现象的原因;

3. 建议一种保持健康的最佳方法,并说明理由。

Part Two Listening Comprehension

Section A

Directions: *In this section you will hear 10 short conversations. At the end of each conversation, a question will be asked about what was said, both the conversation and the question will be spoken only once. After each question there will be a pause. During the pause, you must read the four choices marked A, B, C and D, and decide which is the best answer. Then mark the corresponding letter on the Answer Sheet with a single line through the center.*

1. A. A student.   B. A teacher.

   C. A salesman.   D. A waiter.

2. A. The borrower and lender.

   B. The two librarians.

   C. The librarian and the student.

   D. The teacher and the student.

3. A. In the hotel.   B. At the bus stop.

   C. In the railway station.   D. At the airport.

4. A. Did his homework.   B. Did nothing.

   C. Did his housework.   D. Did a lot of things.

5. A. At 1:30 p.m.   B. At 2:30 p.m.

   C. At 11:00 a.m.   D. At 1:00 p.m.

6. A. At home.   B. At the party.

   C. In the bookstore.   D. In the hospital.

7. A. Bread.   B. Cakes.

   C. Bread and eggs.   D. Eggs.

8. A. Not good.   B. Excellent.

   C. Ugly.   D. Ok.

9. A. Policeman.   B. Waiter.

   C. Cashier.   D. Teacher.

10. A. Open the door.   B. Close the door.

    C. Do nothing.   D. Close the window.

Section B

Directions: *In this section, you will hear three short passages. At the end of each passage, you will hear some questions. Both the passage and the questions will be spoken only once. After you hear a question, you must choose the best answer from the four choices marked A, B, C and D, and decide which is the best answer. Then mark the corresponding letter on the Answer Sheet with a single line through the center.*

Passage One

11. A. In 1861.   B. In 1862.

    C. In 1863.   D. In 1864.

12. A. 2 years.   B. 3 years.

    C. 4 years.   D. 5 years.

13. A. The compromise was made.

    B. The South defeated the North.

    C. The slavery was not abolished.

16

D. The North defeated the South.

Passage Two

14. A. 1. B. 2. C. 3. D. 4.
15. A. 3 years. B. 4 years.
    C. 5 years. D. 6 years.
16. A. 5. B. 4. C. 3. D. 2.

Passage Three

17. A. On December 23.
    B. On December 24.
    C. On December 25.
    D. On December 26.
18. A. Wear new clothes.
    B. Buy the Christmas tree.
    C. Write down their wishes.
    D. Send the cards to their friends.
19. A. Santa Claus. B. Their father.
    C. Their mother. D. Their friends.
20. A. 12 days. B. 13 days.
    C. 17 days. D. 7 days.

Section C

Directions: *In this section, you will hear a passage of about 100 words three times. The passage is printed on your Answer Sheet with about 20 words missing. First you will hear the whole passage from the beginning to the end just to get a general idea of it. Then, in the second reading, you will hear a signal indicating the beginning of a pause after each sentence, sometimes two sentences or just part of a sentence. During the pause, you must write down the missing words you have just heard in the corresponding space on the Answer Sheet. There is also a different signal indicating the end of the pause. When you hear this signal, you must get ready for what comes next from the recording. You can check what you have written when the passage is read to* *you once again without the pauses.*

___(21)___ is located on the ___(22)___ of the Northeastern ___(23)___ at the ___(24)___ of the Hudson River. It has a ___(25)___ of more than ___(26)___ , making it the ___(27)___ city in America by population. It ___(28)___ an area of ___(29)___ square miles.

New York City ___(30)___ ___(31)___ boroughs: Manhattan, Brooklyn, Bronx, Queens and Richmond. The New York Metropolitan Area is ___(32)___ in Manhattan, it is the largest ___(33)___ ___(34)___ of ___(35)___ , finance, ___(36)___ , culture, ___(37)___ in America, even in the ___(38)___ . And ___(39)___ headquarters is also situated in this area.

New York City is popularly known as, "Big Apple", and the "City That Never Sleeps," attracting people from all over the world. By 2006, it is also known for its ___(40)___ crime rate among major cities in the U.S.

Part Three   Reading Comprehension

Section A

Directions: *In this section, there is a passage with 10 blanks. You are required to select one word for each blank from a list of choices given in a word bank following the passage. Read the passage through carefully before making your choices. Each choice in the bank is identified by a letter. Please mark the corresponding letter for each item on Answer Sheet with a single line through the center.* ***You may not use any of words in the bank more than once.***

Word Bank

A. end	C. renamed	E. borough	G. 1885	I. becoming
B. southeast	D. welcome	F. bought	H. buildings	J. said

In New York, Manhattan is a ___(41)___ of New York City in ___(42)___ New York, mainly on Manhattan Island at the north ___(43)___ of New York Bay. It was ___(44)___ that Peter Minuit of the Dutch West Indies Company ___(45)___ the island in 1626 from the Manhattan Indians, supposedly for some $ 24 worth of merchandise. The Island was first named New Amsterdam, and then ___(46)___ New York when the English assumed

18

control in 1664, quickly spread from the southern tip of the island, eventually ___(47)___ the financial, commercial, and cultural center of the United States.

In New York, there are lots of world-famous ___(48)___, such as the Empire State Building, the Statue of Liberty, which is a statue given to the United States by France in ___(49)___, standing at Liberty Island in the mouth of the Hudson River in New York Harbor as a ___(50)___ to all visitors, immigrants, and returning Americans.

Section B

Directions: *There are 2 passages in this section. Each passage is followed by some questions or unfinished statements. For each of them there are four choices marked A, B, C and D. You should decide on the best choice and mark the corresponding letter on Answer Sheet with a single line through the center.*

Passage One

All Americans celebrate the birthday of the United States of America on the fourth of July every year. The fourth of July is called Independence Day. It is a day of picnics and patriotic parades, a night of concerts and fireworks.

It was on July 4, 1776 that United States of America declared her independence. Since then on, the United States of America became an independent country, who was on longer the colony of the United Kingdom. It was on that day that some important people such as George Washington, signed the epoch-making document "the Declaration of Independence". Before they signed this document, the representatives from 13 British colonies were holding the Second Continental Congress. Britain's 13 American colonies, governed by England through the Continental Congress, passed the Declaration of Independence on July 4, 1776. And with John Adams, Benjamin Franklin and Roger Sherman, Thomas Jefferson drafted the Declaration of Independence.

Signing of the Declaration of Independence marked the beginning of American rebellions against British rule and declared that 13 colonies no longer owed loyalties to British King. In 1783, Great Britain signed a formal treaty recognizing the independence of the colonies. This was the end of the Independence Revolution. And on February 4, 1789, George Washington was elected the first President of the United States of America.

Questions 51 to 55 are based on the passage.

51. When is the birthday of USA?

A. On July 3.   B. On July 4.

C. On July 14.   D. On July 15.

52. When was the United States established?

     A. In 1775.   B. In 1776.

     C. In 1777.   D. In 1778.

53. How many states were there when the UAS declared its independence?

     A. 13.   B. 14.   C. 15.   D. 16.

54. Who of the following drafted the Declaration of Independence EXCEPT _____?

     A. John Adams.   B. Roger Sherman.

     C. George Washington.   D. Thomas Jefferson.

55. How long did the Independence War last?

     A. 11 years.   B. 10 years.

     C. 9 years.   D. 8 years.

Passage Two

Slave trade began in the early 1400s on the shore of Africa. The first European slave traders were from Portugal, which dominated the slave trade for about one hundred years. Until 1550s, the Europeans countries challenged the Portuguese. They sent their ships to Africa, followed by the Dutch.

England was no exception and followed suit. It became one of the largest countries to trade slaves. But very soon England became the biggest slave trading nation. England established its first permanent settlement in America at Jamestown, Virginia in 1607. This was the beginning of England's colonization in the New World. By the early 18th century, England replaced Portuguese to become the world biggest slave trader. English people invested a lot in sugar plantations which require laborers. So England sent the slaves to the New World. Although, the colonialists met the stubborn resistance from the slaves, more than 57,000 Africans ware brought to America.

Some people called the slave trade the Triangular Trade because of the ways the ships traveled to form a triangle. The European ships would transport manufactured goods to the Africa. And there they trade guns and other things to the Africans tribes. The tribes would trade the African people captured in the war or other people who broke the law. Sometimes, the Europeans captured the black forcibly and sold them into slavery. Then they carried the slave on the ships bound for （驶往） North America. The

20

ships were terrible because so many slaves were crammed (拥挤) in one ship. They got very little food so that a lot of slaves died of disease or starvation during the journey.

The slave trade lasted for several centuries. Only in the civil War in 1861 was the spread of slavery stopped in the United States.

Questions 56 to 60 are based on the passage.

56. When did the first slave trade begin?

    A. In the early 15th century.

    B. In the early 16th century.

    C. In the early 14th century.

    D. In the early 17th century.

57. Which country was the first to begin the slave trade?

    A. Spain.   B. Netherlands.

    C. America.   D. Portugal.

58. When did England build its first colony in North America?

    A. In 1607.   B. In 1550.

    C. In 1400.   D. In 1861.

59. Why did people call the slave trade the Triangular Trade?

    A. For its benefit.

    B. For its number of slaves.

    C. For the course the ships takes.

    D. For one of the slave traders.

60. What finally led to stopping of the spread of slavery?

    A. African slaves' resistance.

    B. The anti-slavery law.

    C. The European slave traders themselves.

    D. American Civil War.

Part Four   Vocabulary

Directions: *For this part you are required to choose the best answer from A, B, C and D to complete the following sentences.*

61. We were _____ with difficult problems.

    A. faced   B. face   C. facing   D. to face

62. The wounded man found himself _____ on the bed in hospital when he woke up.

    A. lied   B. lie   C. lying   D. to lie

63. During the World War II, her husband was taken _____ by the German soldiers.

    A. prison   B. jail   C. poisoning   D. prisoner

64. The school is only half a mile away _____ my home.

    A. at   B. from   C. in   D. on

65. In the warm weather, he likes leaning _____ the wall outside the house.

    A. against   B. on   C. in   D. with

66. You'll be successful so long as you keep _____ it.

    A. do   B. doing   C. to do   D. being done

67. His wife must pray _____ her husband, expecting him to go back home.

    A. on   B. against   C. at   D. for

68. The thief stared _____ surprise at the policeman in uniform.

    A. in   B. at   C. on   D. with

69. She stood there, with tears _____ down her face.

    A. stream   B. streamed

    C. streaming   D. had streamed

70. He would die _____ he was sent to hospital immediately.

    A. lest   B. but   C. yet   D. unless

71. The twins are _____ with each other, people hardly distinguish one from the other.

    A. familiar   B. similar

    C. identical   D. alike

72. He is a kind person, _____ to help others.

    A. will   B. willed   C. would   D. willing

73. The company supplies food _____ the local people.

    A. for   B. with   C. to   D. at

74. You are _____ the risk to do so.

    A. getting   B. taking

    C. giving   D. wanting

75. Her sudden death has already reported _____ the police.

    A. at   B. in   C. to   D. with

76. He was junior _____ his brother in position.

22

A. as   B. to   C. with   D. as

77. I don't eat a lot because the food is not _____ me.

    A. in line   B. in line for

    C. in line with   D. in line at

78. The officer _____ the soldier to go on marching.

    A. has command   B. have commanded

    C. command   D. commanded

79. He always feels nervous _____ his mother's presence.

    A. at   B. with   C. on   D. in

80. He _____ his reputation as a famous singer.

    A. established   B. establishing

    C. to establish   D. have established

Part Five   Short Answer Questions

Directions: *In this part there is a short passage with five questions or incomplete state-ments. Read the passage carefully. Then answer the questions or complete the statement in the fewest possible words.*

Today, the United States of America is a powerful nation in the world both econom-ically and culturally. It is a nation originally made of immigrants, who came not only from Europe and Asia, but also from Africa. So compared to the population in other countries, the population in America is most racially and culturally diverse in the world. Just for that reason, America is also called a "Melting pot". But until now, there is still a social problem existing in today's America, that is, the racial discrimination, especially against the black.

Although the Civil War ended in abolishing (废除) of the slavery in the south in 1865, the black people were still discriminated by the white. In public, they were pro-hibited to use the same bus or eat at the same restaurant with the white people. They are still heavily segregated. So immediately after the Civil War, blacks throughout the South organized mass meetings and conventions demanding equality before the law, the right to vote, and equal access to schools, transportation, and other public facilities. Although the segregation is commonly associated with the south, *segregation* can be found in every part of that country. For example, a black people in Boston sued to allow the city of

Boston to allow her daughter to attend the nearest the school, instead of faraway segregated school. Finally the black man lost this case, but the local black benefited a lot when the state legislature prohibited segregation in public.

Martin Luther King, Jr. born on Jan. 15, 1929, was one of the famous leaders of Civil Rights Movement in America. He led a massive protest against segregations, requiring that Negro and white rode buses as equals. In 1964, he was awarded Nobel Peace Prize, and became the youngest man in the world to receive the Noble Peace Prize. But on the evening of April 4, 1968, when he was ready to lead a protest march in sympathy with striking garbage workers of that city, he was assassinated.

81. Why do people call United States of America a "melting pot"?

82. What does the word "segregation" in 2nd paragraph mean?

83. Martin Luther King, Jr. won the Noble Peach Prize at the age of _____.

84. When did Martin Luther King, Jr. die? And how?

85. What's your attitude toward the racial discrimination in America?

Part Six   Translation

Directions: *Finish the sentences on Answer Sheet by translating into English.*

86. 听到这个消息以后,他勃然大怒。(flare)

87. 她的工作是会后将会议内容写下来。(write out)

88. 他们去除了很多过时的概念。(brush aside)

89. 紧急救助使杰克脱离了危险。(bring through)

90. 我有一些好朋友过去一直和我站在一边,现在还是。(stand by)

91. 困兽犹斗。(fight back)

92. 他走进屋里,然后瘫倒在我的怀里。(stumble)

93. 玛丽终于查明了那天晚上发生事情的真相。(find out)

94. 你最好尽快去看医生,否则,你的伤口会感染。(infect)

95. 他被敌人抓住了,并在监狱里度过了他的余生。(capture)

Answer Sheet 1

Part One   Writing

_____

_____

_____

_____

_____

_____

_____

_____

_____

_____

_____

_____

_____

_____

_____

_____

_____

_____

_____

_____

Part Two   Listening Comprehension

Section C

_____(21)_____ is located on the _____(22)_____ of the Northeastern _____(23)_____ at the _____(24)_____ of the Hudson River. It has a _____(25)_____ of more than _____(26)_____ , making it the _____(27)_____ city in America by population. It _____(28)_____ an area of _____(29)_____ square miles.

New York City _____(30)_____ _____(31)_____ boroughs: Manhattan, Brooklyn, Bronx, Queens and Richmond. The New York Metropolitan Area is _____(32)_____ in Manhattan, it is the largest _____(33)_____ _____(34)_____ of _____(35)_____ , finance, _____(36)_____ , culture, _____(37)_____ in America, even in the _____(38)_____ . And _____(39)_____ headquarters is also situated in this area.

New York City is popularly known as, "Big Apple", and the "City That Never Sleeps," attracting people from all over the world. By 2006, it is also known for its _____(40)_____ crime rate among major cities in the U.S.

Part Five   Short Answer Questions

81. _____

_____

82. _____

_____

83. _____

_____

84. _____

_____

85. _____

_____

Part Six   Translation

86. _____

_____

_____

87. _____

88.

89.

90.

91.

92.

93.

94.

95.

Answer Sheet 2

Part Two   Listening Comprehension
Section A

1	2	3	4	5	6	7	8	9	10

Section B

11	12	13	14	15	16	17	18	19	20

Part Three   Reading Comprehension
Section A

41	42	43	44	45	46	47	48	49	50

Section B

51	52	53	54	55	56	57	58	59	60

Part Four   Vocabulary

61	62	63	64	65	66	67	68	69	70

71	72	73	74	75	76	77	78	79	80

Model Test 3

Part One   Writing

Directions: *For this part, you are allowed 30 minutes to write a composition on the topic given in English. You should write at least 100 words.*

My Favorite Teacher

1. 描述一下你最喜欢的老师；
2. 通过一两件小事情,来展现你最喜欢的老师优点或对你的影响；
3. 表达自己对老师的祝愿。

Part Two   Listening Comprehension

Section A

Directions: *In this section you will hear 10 short conversations. At the end of each conversation, a question will be asked about what was said, both the conversation and the question will be spoken only once. After each question there will be a pause. During the pause, you must read the four choices marked A, B, C and D, and decided which is the best answer. Then mark the corresponding letter on the Answer Sheet with a single line through the center.*

1. A. Traffic jam.   B. Overslept.
   C. Forgot to do so.   D. Not clear.
2. A. In the restaurant.   B. In the office.
   C. In the library.   D. At home.
3. A. Stay at home.   B. Do her homework.
   C. Do nothing.   D. Go to see a film.
4. A. In her pocket.   B. At home.
   C. In the drawer.   D. On the desk.

5. A. Sunny.   B. Cloudy.

   C. Rainy.   D. Overcast.

6. A. Bigger.   B. Big.

   C. Small.   D. Medium.

7. A. Go to the cinema.

   B. Go to the supermarket.

   C. Have a supper.

   D. Go home.

8. A. To be a teacher.

   B. Go on with his study.

   C. He doesn't know.

   D. Find a job.

9. A. Wait for Jack.

   B. Wait for Jacket's call.

   C. Call Jack again.

   D. Write an E-mail to Jack.

10. A. No.   B. Yes.

    C. Not sure.   D. Maybe.

Section B

Directions: *In this section, you will hear three short passages. At the end of each passage, you will hear some questions. Both the passage and the questions will be spoken only once. After you hear a question, you must choose the best answer from the four choices marked A, B, C and D, and decide which is the best answer. Then mark the corresponding letter on the Answer Sheet with a single line through the center.*

Passage One

11. A. On the 15th of October.

    B. On the 5th of October.

    C. On the 5th of September.

    D. On the 15th of September.

12. A. On the 15th of September.

B. On the 5th of October.

C. On the 5th of September.

D. On the 15th of October.

13. A. On the 10th of September.

B. On the 11th of September.

C. On the 12th of September.

D. On the 13th of September.

Passage Two

14. A. 3.   B. 4.   C. 5.   D. 6.

15. A. Patience.   B. To be strict with students.

C. Energy.   D. Knowledge.

16. A. Patience.   B. Passionate.

C. Knowledge.   D. To be strict with students.

Passage Three

17. A. In 1635.   B. In 1636.

C. In 1637.   D. In 1638.

18. A. In 1638.   B. In 1637.

C. In 1636.   D. In 1635.

19. A. 6.   B. 7.   C. 8.   D. 9.

20. A. 8.   B. 9.   C. 10.   D. 11.

Section C

Directions: *In this section, you will hear a passage of about 100 words three times. The passage is printed on your Answer Sheet with about 20 words missing. First you will hear the whole passage from the beginning to the end just to get a general idea of it. Then, in the second reading, you will hear a signal indicating the beginning of a pause after each sentence, sometimes two sentences or just part of a sentence. During the pause, you must write down the missing words you have just heard in the corresponding space on the Answer Sheet. There is also a different signal indicating the end of the pause. When you hear this signal, you must get ready for what comes next from the*

31

recording. You can check what you have written when the passage is read to you once again without the pauses.

American __(21)__ system is quite __(22)__ from Chinese education __(23)__ . In most areas in __(24)__ , the __(25)__ education begins with the __(26)__ classes for the five-year-odd children. The children usually __(27)__ half a day __(28)__ classes in there. For the children from three to five, they may __(29)__ to go to the __(30)__ schools or day care __(31)__ . That is __(32)__ education. When a child is about __(33)__ years old, he or she will __(34)__ first grade. There are __(35)__ grades for him or her to __(36)__ . The grade one to grade eight is called __(37)__ school, and the grade nine to grade twelve is called __(38)__ . A high school __(39)__ may go to __(40)__ if his test scores are good enough to be admitted to one college or university.

Part Three Reading Comprehension

Section A

Directions: *In this section, there is a passage with 10 blanks. You are required to select one word for each blank from a list of choices given in a word bank following the passage. Read the passage through carefully before making your choices. Each choice in the bank is identified by a letter. Please mark the corresponding letter for each item on Answer Sheet with a single line through the center.* **You may not use any of words in the bank more than once.**

Word Bank

A. for	C. recognition	E. European	G. graduated	I. who
B. said	D. considered	F. born	H. widely	J. influential

Ralph Waldo Emerson, was __(41)__ in Boston in1803. At the age of **17**, he __(42)__ from Harvard University and taught there for a short time. Then he left school and began his journey in __(43)__ continents. He spent most of his time in Italy and England. His first work was *Nature*, published in 1836, which gained little __(44)__ . But he made his name in his essay entitled *Self-Reliance*. In his works, Emerson shows that he believed in individualism, and self-reliance. And __(45)__ this reason, he was __(46)__ as the leader of the movement-Transcendentalism. It was __(47)__ that it was

32

Emerson __(48)__ brought this movement to New England. So he is __(49)__ regarded as the most __(50)__ philosophers, essayist, and the leader of the Transcendentalism.

Section B

Directions: *There are 2 passages in this section. Each passage is followed by some questions or unfinished statements. For each of them there are four choices marked A, B, C and D. You should decide on the best choice and mark the corresponding letter on Answer Sheet with a single line through the center.*

Passage One

Confucius was born in the village of Zou in the state of Lu (in today's Qufu, Shandong province), on September, 28, 551 B. C. His Chinese name was Kong Zi. He was one of famous philosophers, thinkers and educators in ancient China. His father, commander of a district in the country of Lu passed away three years after Confucius was born. So the whole family was in real anguish. But he was lucky enough to receive fine education.

Later he became a good teacher. He acquired such a reputation as a teacher that he was appointed to a position in the government, and eventually became Minister of Public Works and then Minister of Crime at the age of fifty. But his ideas and thought *ran counter to* those of the rulers and the government, he finally resigned and devoted himself to teaching.

During his study and teaching, he founded the school called the Ru School of Chinese thought or Confucianism. Confucianism has exerted great influence on Chinese history and culture and even largely influenced the culture of Korea, Japan. His teaching and thoughts were mainly preserved in *the Analects*. In this book, Confucius made many wise sayings in ancient China that helped many people learn about nature, the world, and their manners. He also helped the government and the emperor by teaching them lessons on how the emperor should rule his kingdom successfully. So Confucianism became the basis of the Chinese State during the Han Dynasty (206 BC - 220 AD).

He also did greatest contributions to Chinese history. He edited, compiled or wrote the 'Five Classics' and the 'Four Books' which contain the morals and philosophy that the Chinese people have followed consistently for the past 2500 years. In these books, he put forward five important relationships: Ruler to minister; Father to son; Husband to wife; Older brother to Younger brother; Friend to friend. This is the core of Confucian thoughts.

Confucius spent a lot of years wandering in china with his ideas. He eventually returned to Lu at age 67. Although he was welcomed there and chose to remain, he was not offered public office again, nor did he seek it. Instead he spent the rest of his years teaching and, finally, writing. He died at 72.

51. When did Confucius' father die?

　　A. In 550 B.C.　　　　　　　　B. In 549 B.C.

　　C. In 548 B.C.　　　　　　　　D. In 547 B.C.

52. When did Confucius become the Minister of Crime?

　　A. In 499 B.C.　　　　　　　　B. In 500 B.C.

　　C. In 501 B.C.　　　　　　　　D. In 501 B.C.

53. What does the phrase "**ran counter to**" mean in paraphrase 2?

　　A. Were opposite to.　　　　　　B. Were different from.

　　C. Disagreed with.　　　　　　　D. Disliked.

54. Which book were Confucius's thoughts kept in?

　　A. *Five Classics*.　　　　　　　B. *The Analects*.

　　C. *Four Books*.　　　　　　　　D. *Confucianism*.

55. How many important relationships did Confucius raise in his books?

　　A. 2.　　　　　　　　　　　　　B. 3.

　　C. 4.　　　　　　　　　　　　　D. 5.

Passage Two

Ivy League refers to an association of eight universities and colleges in the northeast United States. They are Harvard University, Princeton University, Yale University, Columbia University, Cornell University, Brown University, University of Pennsylvania, Dartmouth University. All these universities and colleges are private ones, with high academic and social prestige. According to the rankings of U.S. News & World Report, the eight universities and colleges are among TOP 14 universities and Princeton University takes the lead, followed by Harvard University and Yale University ranks the third.

Why is it called "Ivy"? The name dates back to the year of 1937, one of the New York reporter found that the old buildings of the 8 universities in the northeast United

States were covered with ivy. So he coined the term "Ivy League", referring to those 8 universities. Then the term was officially by the Council of Ivy Group Presidents. And the Ivy League was established 19 years after the term was first used.

Questions 56 to 60 are based on the passage.

56. How many universities does Ivy League include?

    A. 8.   B. 9.   C. 10.   D. 11.

57. What kind of universities are those universities in Ivy League?

    A. Run by Federal government.

    B. State universities.

    C. Public.

    D. Private.

58. According to the rankings of U. S. News & World Report, which university ranks the second among American universities?

    A. Yale University.   B. Harvard University.

    C. Princeton University.   D. Columbia University.

59. When was the name "Ivy League" first used?

    A. In 1935.   B. In 1936.

    C. In 1937.   D. In 1938.

60. When was the Ivy League established?

    A. In 1953.   B. In 1954.

    C. In 1955.   D. In 1956.

Part Four　Vocabulary

Directions: *For this part you are required to choose the best answer from A, B, C and D to complete the following sentences.*

61. I attempted _____ the CET 4, but failed at last.

    A. pass   B. have passed   C. passing   D. to pass

62. Nowadays, people feel that it is more and more difficult to _____ their living in the big cities.

    A. get   B. earn   C. get   D. try

63. I was very tired because I stayed _____ preparing for my lesson last night.

    A. up   B. on   C. in   D. by

64. I was very _____ when he told that news.

    A. amaze

    B. amazing

    C. amazed

    D. amazingly

65. As a teacher, Mary feels that she is _____ to share what she knows with her students.

    A. compel

    B. compelling

    C. compels

    D. compelled

66. Don't disturb him, he is _____ notes on what he reads in the books.

    A. getting

    B. having

    C. making

    D. taking

67. Jack improves very quickly because he has taken up the habit of _____ diaries.

    A. keeping

    B. having

    C. making

    D. writing

68. It is generally believed that true love is built _____ mutual understanding.

    A. in   B. at   C. up   D. on

69. I'm afraid that I can't _____ the loan because I have no cash in hand.

    A. repay   B. repaid   C. paid   D. pay

70. He leaves _____ a "p" in the word "opportunity".

    A. off   B. out   C. on   D. at

71. Elizabeth is a very excellent student. She finally wins a fellowship _____ Peking University.

    A. for   B. to   C. with   D. at

72. Michael first majored in English, but then he switched _____ law.

    A. to   B. in   C. at   D. with

73. The man is very _____ in repairing computers.

    A. interesting

    B. disinterested

    C. interested

    D. uninteresting

74. He stopped reading the novel and went on _____ a picture.

    A. drew   B. draw   C. drawing   D. to draw

75. We should learn _____ analysis rather than _____ intuition.

    A. by, by   B. on, by   C. by, of   D. for, of

76. He asks, "what is the point _____ so?"

    A. do   B. of doing   C. to do   D. doing

77. When the beast is coming, all people _____ their breath.

    A. keep   B. catch   C. take   D. breathe

78. He has a lot of hobbies, for example, he enjoys _____ the stamps.

    A. /   B. collect

    C. collecting   D. to collect

79. A good teacher must be good at _____ his students in class.

    A. simulate   B. simulating

    C. stimulate   D. stimulating

80. He was _____ by the hard questions, not knowing how to answer them.

    A. puzzled   B. puzzling

    C. to puzzle   D. puzzle

Part Five   Short Answer Questions

Directions: *In this part there is a short passage with five questions or incomplete statements. Read the passage carefully. Then answer the questions or complete the statement in the fewest possible words.*

Occupational disease is a kind of disease or disability resulting from conditions of employment (usually from long exposure to a noxious substance or from continuous repetition of certain acts).

This kind of disease is closely linked to the workplace. The following workplaces can cause an occupational disease: dust, gases, or fumes; noise; toxic substances (poisons); radiation; infectious germs or viruses; extreme hot or cold temperatures. Those workplaces can lead to different reactions in people's body: first, Immediate or acute reactions, like shortness of breath or nausea, can be caused by a one-time event, (e.g., a chemical spill). These reactions are not usually permanent. Second, Gradual reactions, like asthma (哮喘)or dermatitis(皮炎) (skin rashes), can get worse and persist when you are exposed over days, weeks or months. These reactions tend to last for a longer time. Third, delayed reactions or diseases that take a long time to develop, like lung cancer or loss of hearing, can be caused by long-term exposure to a substance or work activity. These reactions can be noticed long after the job is over.

The teacher also faces some occupational diseases, though they are not as serious as those of the above-mentioned ones. A study shows that occupational voice disorders accounts for over 25% of all occupational diseases in teachers. This is the most common occupational disease. For the teachers, the most dangerous threat is the chalk dust or marker fumes.

So your workplace should be healthy for your body and mind. You can help to keep yourself and your workplace healthy by being aware of health hazards(危险) in your environment.

81. To explain what is occupational disease in your own words. And give one or two examples.

82. How many reactions does the author list here in people's body? And sum up them.

83. What is the most common occupational disease for the teachers?

84. What does greatest harm to the teacher's body?

85. What's your suggestion on the teacher's occupational disease?

Part Six   Translation

Directions: *Finish the sentences on Answer Sheet by translating into English.*

86. 他今天感到很累,因为他昨天一夜没睡看世界杯。(stay up)

87. 现在关键问题是学生们不知道在课堂上如何记笔记。(take notes)

88. 他现在的成功是建立在他不断努力的基础之上的。(build on)

89. 学生应该养成写日记的好习惯。(keep a diary)

90. 我们不应该只考虑这一个因素,而遗漏了其他重要的因素。(leave out)

91. 你能帮我明天把这个包裹寄给我的朋友吗?(send off)

92. 恐怕他们不能来参加我们的婚礼了,因为他们正在从事一项新的发明。(work at)

93. 会场的每个人都屏住了的呼吸等待结果的宣布。(catch one's breath)

94. 我相信中国队一定会在接下来的比赛中取胜。(convince)

95. 这要求我们思考一下他对家乡所做出的贡献。(reflect)

Answer Sheet 1

Part One   Writing

_____

_____

_____

_____

_____

_____

_____

_____

_____

_____

_____

_____

_____

_____

_____

_____

_____

_____

_____

_____

_____

Part Two   Listening Comprehension

Section C

American __(21)__ system is quite __(22)__ from Chinese education __(23)__ . In most areas in __(24)__ , the __(25)__ education begins with the __(26)__ classes for the five-year-odd children. The children usually __(27)__ half a day __(28)__ classes in there. For the children from three to five, they may __(29)__ to go to the __(30)__ schools or day care __(31)__ . That is __(32)__ education. When a child is about __(33)__ years old, he or she will __(34)__ first grade. There are __(35)__ grades for him or her to __(36)__ . The grade one to grade eight is called __(37)__ school, and the grade nine to grade twelve is called __(38)__ . A high school __(39)__ may go to __(40)__ if his test scores are good enough to be admitted to one college or university.

Part Five   Short Answer Questions

81. _____

_____

82. _____

_____

83. _____

_____

84. _____

_____

85. _____

_____

Part Six   Translation

86. _____

_____

87. _____

_____

_____

88. _____

_____

_____

89. _____

_____

_____

90. _____

_____

_____

91. _____

_____

_____

92. _____

_____

_____

93. _____

_____

_____

94. _____

_____

_____

95. _____

_____

_____

Answer Sheet 2

Part Two   Listening Comprehension
Section A

1	2	3	4	5	6	7	8	9	10

Section B

11	12	13	14	15	16	17	18	19	20

Part Three   Reading Comprehension
Section A

41	42	43	44	45	46	47	48	49	50

Section B

51	52	53	54	55	56	57	58	59	60

Part Four   Vocabulary

61	62	63	64	65	66	67	68	69	70
71	72	73	74	75	76	77	78	79	80

Model Test 4

Part One   Writing

Directions: *For this part, you are allowed 30 minutes to write a composition on the topic given in English. You should write at least 100 words.*

My Attitude toward Beggars

1. 目前大城市大街小巷有一些沿街乞讨者；
2. 你如何看待这一社会问题；
3. 提出几个解决这一问题的方案。

Part Two   Listening Comprehension

Section A

Directions: *In this section you will hear 10 short conversations. At the end of each conversation, a question will be asked about what was said, both the conversation and the question will be spoken only once. After each question there will be a pause. During the pause, you must read the four choices marked A, B, C and D, and decide which is the best answer. Then mark the corresponding letter on the Answer sheet with a single line through the center.*

1. A. Salesman.
   C. Waiter
   B. Hotel receptionist.
   D. A house agent.

2. A. In the library.
   C. In the restaurant.
   B. In the office.
   D. At home.

3. A. On Wednesday.
   C. On Thursday.
   B. On Monday.
   D. On Friday.

4. A. At Mike's home.
   B. At Jack's home.

C. At Mary's home.

D. In the classroom.

5. A. In 2003.   B. In 2002.

   C. In 2000.   D. In 2001.

6. A. He has been there.

   B. He plans to go there.

   C. He has enough money.

   D. He has not enough money.

7. A. 3 million.   B. 4 million.

   C. 4.3 million.   D. 3.4 million.

8. A. In July.   B. In May.

   C. In March.   D. In June.

9. A. By train.   B. By bus.

   C. By boat.   D. By air.

10. A. Next Tuesday.

    B. Tomorrow.

    C. Wednesday.

    D. this weekend.

Section B

Directions: *In this section, you will hear three short passages. At the end of each passage, you will hear some questions. Both the passage and the questions will be spoken only once. After you hear a question, you must choose the best answer from the four choices marked A, B, C and D, and decide which is the best answer. Then mark the corresponding letter on the Answer Sheet with a single line through the center.*

Passage One

11. A. 2.8 million.   B. 1.2 million.

    C. 2.8 billion.   D. 1.2 billion.

12. A. 2.8 million.   B. 1.2 million.

    C. 2.8 billion.   D. 1.2 billion.

13. A. 8.   B. 9.   C. 14.   D. 15.

Passage Two

14. A. 25,000.   B. 2,500.
    C. 250,000.   D. 25 million.
15. A. 1.   B. 2.   C. 3.   D. 4.
16. A. Money.   B. Work.
    C. Relief.   D. Education.

Passage Three

17. A. In 1943.   B. In 1935.
    C. In 1925.   D. In 1945.
18. A. 20.34%.   B. 21.34%.
    C. 21.43%.   D. 23.14%.
19. A. More than 1.1 billion.
    B. 1.1 billion.
    C. More than 1.01 billion.
    D. 1.01 billion.
20. A. 1/3.   B. 1/5.
    C. 1/4.   D. 1/6.

Section C

Directions: *In this section, you will hear a passage of about 100 words three times. The passage is printed on your Answer Sheet with about 20 words missing. First you will hear the whole passage from the beginning to the end just to get a general idea of it. Then, in the second reading, you will hear a signal indicating the beginning of a pause after each sentence, sometimes two sentences or just part of a sentence. During the pause, you must write down the missing words you have just heard in the corresponding space on the Answer Sheet. There is also a different signal indicating the end of the pause. When you hear this signal, you must get ready for what comes next from the recording. You can check what you have written when the passage is read to you once again without the pauses.*

It is __(21)__ to see __(22)__ or the homeless __(23)__ on the ground begging for money in the big cites like Beijing, Shanghai etc. Some __(24)__ people, usually the __(25)__ women in large cities make a __(26)__ by collecting __(27)__ drink bottles. Every day, they __(28)__ for the drink bottles from one dust bin to another. Some of the __(29)__ may give out some money to those __(30)__ people or the disabled. But recent reports from the __(31)__ that some of the beggars are not real beggars, they either lead a __(32)__ life after "working hours", or __(33)__ to be as poor as the __(34)__ . So when people __(35)__ the help, they feel being __(36)__ sometimes. But basically they are very __(37)__ . If you don't __(38)__ the food in the __(39)__ , you may __(40)__ them up and give them to the poor, or the homeless you meet.

Part Three Reading Comprehension

Section A

Directions: *In this section, there is a passage with 10 blanks. You are required to select one word for each blank from a list of choices given in a word bank following the passage. Read the passage through carefully before making your choices. Each choice in the bank is identified by a letter. Please mark the corresponding letter for each item on Answer Sheet with a single line through the center.* **You may not use any of words in the bank more than once.**

Word Bank

A. role	C. compulsive	E. decreases	G. less	I. illiterate
B. access	D. out of	F. intelligence.	H. founding	J. invests

Education plays an important __(41)__ in lifting people __(42)__ poverty. Every year, Chinese government __(43)__ a lot of fund into the education. Since the __(44)__ of People's Republic of China in 1949, more and more people have gained __(45)__ to education. In particular, after the nine-year __(46)__ education policy was carried out all over the country, the number of the __(47)__ and semi-literate __(48)__ dramatically. The more education people receive, the __(49)__ likely they are to become poor. Thus it can lead to the enhancement of the __(50)__ level in our country.

Section B

Directions: *There are 2 passages in this section. Each passage is followed by some ques-*

Passage One

China's "Project Hope" is a public welfare project initiated and developed by China Youth Development Foundation from October 1989 which aims to help children of impoverished(穷困的) regions continue their study in primary schools and improve the education environment in there areas.

Because of the historical reasons, people in different parts of China can't equally enjoy the same right of education because a lot of people in the remote areas, mainly in China's underdeveloped middle and western regions can't afford the expenses of the schooling. Although the government has invested a lot of money into those areas, it is still too little to support all of the students to go back to school. It was under such a circumstance that the authorities concerned carried out this "Project Hope".

According to the statistics from Xinhua News Agency, Project Hope has helped more than 3.04 million dropouts return to school across China since it was launched 18 years ago. A total of 13,285 Project Hope schools have been built with financing from the scheme in the country's faraway and mountainous regions. The project has received more than 2.2 billion yuan (about 265 million US dollars) of domestic and overseas donations. These funds have been used in the renovation and building of Project Hope primary schools, said an official of the China Youth Development Foundation, which is responsible for the operation of the project.

By far, Project Hope has become the largest and most influential non-government welfare project in China.

Questions 51 to 55 are based on the passage.

51. When was the Project Hope launched in China?

    A. In 1986.   B. In 1987.

    C. In 1988.   D. In 1989.

52. What kind of schools does the Project Hope mainly finance?

    A. High schools.   B. Primary schools.

    C. Middle schools.   D. Colleges.

53. How many pupils have the Project Hope helped to return their schools?

    A. 13,285.   B. 2.3 million.

    C. 3.04 million.   D. 2.2 billion.

54. Project Hope primary schools are mainly located in _____?

    A. the middle and western regions

    B. the middle regions

    C. the western regions

    D. the southern regions

55. Where does the fund of Project Hope mainly come from?

    A. Chinese government.

    B. Domestic and overseas donations.

    C. China Youth Development Foundation.

    D. Provincial governments.

Passage Two

"Spring Bud Program" is a program initiated and organized by China Children and Teenagers' Fund (CCTF) in 1989. It is implemented for aiding the girls in poor areas in returning to school. Because of the limitations of natural conditions, the imbalance of social, economic and cultural development, especially traditional practices in China, the female illiteracy accounts for over two-thirds of the total. Girls are very often deprived of educational opportunities by their parents, due to poverty and gender bias in rural areas. To help those dropout girls, the program was launched.

According to the statistics from China Children and Teenagers' Fund, in the past 18 years, the Spring Bud Program has successfully helped more than 1.7 million girls in China. Since 1989, CCTF has built more than 500 schools for Spring Bud girls.

Recently, the Spring Bud Project has extended its scope by focusing more attention on girls' vocational training. CCTF has set up Practical Skills Training program for the women. Huge numbers of young women now benefit a lot form this program. Now, the Spring Bud Project turns to help the single-parent families in the urban areas.

Questions 56 to 60 are based on the passage.

56. Who organized the Spring Bud Program?

    A. A businessman.

B. China Children and Teenagers' Fund.

C. All-China Women's Federation.

D. The State Council.

57. Which of the following is NOT the reason to lead to dropout of the girls in rural areas?

A. Government's support.

B. Social imbalance.

C. Economic imbalance.

D. Poor natural condition.

58. How many years has the Spring Bud Program been carried out up to 2008?

A. 18.   B. 17.

C. 19.   D. 16.

59. How many girls have got the help from the Spring Bud Program in China?

A. 1.7 million.   B. 500 million.

C. 1 million.   D. 1.6 million.

60. Which of the following is NOT the scope of the Spring Bud Program?

A. Girls in rural areas.

B. Girls in big cities.

C. Girls from the single-parent families.

D. Girls without practical skills in poor areas.

Part Four   Vocabulary

Directions: *For this part you are required to choose the best answer from A, B, C and D to complete the following sentences.*

61. You always find some poor people _____ on the streets in the cities.

A. have wandered   B. wandering

C. wandered   D. to wander

62. Nowadays, some people tend to lead an _____ life.

A. isolate   B. isolating

C. isolated   D. to isolate

63. My brother was _____ and out. So I had to help him out of trouble.

A. up   B. in   C. down   D. inside

64. _____ most cases, the home won the game in the final.

A. In   B. At   C. Up   D. On

65. The man said he lost his appetite _____ the food, but he ate three bowls of rice

for supper yesterday.

 A. at   B. upon

 C. for   D. on

66. Neither _____ interested in this film we saw yesterday.

 A. they   B. they are

 C. are they   D. was they

67. It's really annoying. It rained for several days _____ end.

 A. on   B. in   C. in   D. by

68. I didn't notice her when she passed me _____ on the street.

 A. in   B. by   C. up   D. on

69. I believe I'm qualified for this job. But I don't know how to _____ for this posi-

tion.

 A. take   B. applied C. apply   D. pay

70. The boss let me go and turn the salesman _____.

 A. away   B. out   C. on   D. at

71. In _____, men are better at directions than women.

 A. generally   B. generalize

 C. generalization   D. general

72. He took what he said at the meeting _____ a threat.

 A. as   B. in   C. at   D. with

73. Because _____ his hard work, he achieved great success in the end.

 A. as   B. in   C. at   D. of

74. Don't eat that apple, it was _____.

 A. rot   B. rotten

 C. rotting   D. to rot

75. My computer broke down yesterday. I have it _____ today.

 A. fixed   B. being fixed

 C. fix   D. to fix

76. He had told me what had happened _____ him.

 A. to   B. of   C. /   D. with

77. He spent five minutes _____ this article.

A. finish B. to finish

C. finished D. finishing

78. He is the man who can't _____ the sheep from the goats.

A. / B. tell

C. separate D. say

79. The government is trying to do _____ she can to help the poor people.

A. which B. when

C. what D. where

80. There is a gradual _____ of focus from development of agriculture to the economic construction.

A. shift B. move

C. drift D. lift

Part Five   Short Answer Questions

Directions: *In this part there is a short passage with five questions or incomplete statements. Read the passage carefully. Then answer the questions or complete the statement in the fewest possible words.*

The Chinese government decided to carry out the Western China Development strategy to develop central and western China in 2000. The western and central part of China includes 12 provinces and autonomous regions. It covers an area of 6.58 million square kilometers with a population of 3.67 hundred million, roughly 28.8% of the total population in China. The large scale development of West China is of profound significance.

The central government has taken plentiful measures to promote the development of those areas. It has implemented preferential policies and invested billions of dollars to improve the region's infrastructure, environment and economy. A batch of huge projects including railways, power transmission, and gas pipelines has been launched there to exploit tourism, energy and minerals. The priority should be given to improving the region's environment and infrastructure. The State Council has called on the country's underdeveloped western regions to promote sustainable economic and social development.

The western and central regions should also seize the opportunity of the country's initiative in developing the region to achieve economic prosperity. And they must give full play to its rich agricultural, livestock and energy resources and to continue to improve farming and develop cash products. Those areas should step up efforts in infrastructure construction and make better and more rational use of its natural resources, such as water, farmland, and mineral resources.

In addition, the west areas' unique unfavorable geographic positions greatly limit its development. And if left unchanged, the underdevelopment in the west will greatly affect overall prosperity and even social stability. But it calls for tremendous efforts of several generations. As the result of the great project, the central and western regions of China will surely achieve better and faster development in the future.

81. By 2008, how many years have the Western China strategy been carried out in China?

82. What should be paid special attention in developing western regions?

83. To sum up what efforts the Chinese government should make to develop western and central areas.

84. To sum up what efforts the western and central areas should make.

85. What's Western China Development strategy?

Part Six   Translation

Directions: *Finish the sentences on Answer Sheet by translating into English.*

86. 他喜欢各种各样的运动,尤其是橄榄球。(keen on)

87. 年轻人应该尽量赶上时代的步伐。(keep up)

88. 这座火山有时候会爆发。(once in a while)

89. 一般来说,刻苦努力的人更容易成功。(in general)

90. 政府已经采取措施处理这些棘手的社会问题。(cope with)

91. 不管发生什么事情,我都支持你。(no matter what)

92. 我不明白他在论坛上说的那些话(at a loss)

93. 优惠券的持有人可在本店享受打折优惠。(be entitled to)

94. 你考虑得很周全,谢谢你为我们安排这次旅行。(considerate)

95. 他声称这种药能治愈癌症。(claim)

Answer Sheet 1

Part One   Writing

_____

_____

_____

_____

_____

_____

_____

_____

_____

_____

_____

_____

_____

_____

_____

_____

_____

_____

_____

_____

_____

_____

_____

Part Two Listening Comprehension

Section C

It is __(21)__ to see __(22)__ or the homeless __(23)__ on the ground begging for money in the big cites like Beijing, Shanghai etc. Some __(24)__ poor people, usually the __(25)__ women in large cities make a __(26)__ by collecting __(27)__ drink bottles. Every day, they __(28)__ for the drink bottles from one dust bin to another. Some of the __(29)__ may give out some money to those __(30)__ people or the disabled. But recent reports from the __(31)__ that some of the beggars are not real beggars, they either lead a __(32)__ life after "working hours", or __(33)__ to be as poor as the __(34)__ . So when people __(35)__ the help, they feel being __(36)__ sometimes. But basically they are very __(37)__ . If you don't __(38)__ the food in the __(39)__ , you may __(40)__ them up and give them to the poor, or the homeless you meet.

Part Five Short Answer Questions

81. _____

_____

82. _____

_____

83. _____

_____

84. _____

_____

85. _____

_____

Part Six Translation

86. _____

_____

_____

87. _____

_____

88. _____

89. _____

90. _____

91. _____

92. _____

93. _____

94. _____

95. _____

Answer Sheet 2

Part Two Listening Comprehension
Section A

1	2	3	4	5	6	7	8	9	10

Section B

11	12	13	14	15	16	17	18	19	20

Part Three Reading Comprehension
Section A

41	42	43	44	45	46	47	48	49	50

Section B

51	52	53	54	55	56	57	58	59	60

Part Four Vocabulary

61	62	63	64	65	66	67	68	69	70
71	72	73	74	75	76	77	78	79	80

Model Test 5

Part One   Writing

Directions: *For this part, you are allowed 30 minutes to write a composition on the topic given in English. You should write at least 100 words.*

What I have learned from My Mother

1. 从外表、性格、人品等方面,简要介绍一下你的母亲;
2. 你从母亲身上学到了哪些优点(做人的道理、性格的塑造等);
3. 表达对母亲的祝愿和感谢。

Part Two   Listening Comprehension

Section A

Directions: *In this section you will hear 10 short conversations. At the end of each conversation, a question will be asked about what was said, both the conversation and the question will be spoken only once. After each question there will be a pause. During the pause, you must read the four choices marked A, B, C and D, and decide which is the best answer. Then mark the corresponding letter on the Answer sheet with a single line through the center.*

1. A. On Sunday.   B. On Tuesday.
   C. On Thursday.   D. On Wednesday.
2. A. By bike.   B. By bus.
   C. By subway.   D. By taxi.
3. A. 2.   B. 1.   C. 3.   D. 4.
4. A. A teacher.   B. A manager.
   C. A doctor.   D. A student.
5. A. 0:2.   B. 2:3.

C. 1:5.   D. 0:5.

6. A. At 10:30.   B. At 8:30.

   C. At 11:30.   D. At 9:30.

7. A. He got a low salary.

   B. He made mistakes.

   C. The bad working condition.

   D. He didn't like the job at all.

8. A. 15 years.   B. 5 years.

   C. 13 years.   D. 50 years.

9. A. None of them.   B. Her dad's.

   C. John's.   D. Her mother's.

10. A. The policeman.

    B. The taxi driver.

    C. The doctor.

    D. The teacher.

Section B

Directions: *In this section, you will hear three short passages. At the end of each pas-*
sage, you will hear some questions. Both the passage and the questions will
be spoken only once. After you hear a question, you must choose the best an-
swer from the four choices marked A, B, C and D, and decide which is the
best answer. Then mark the corresponding letter on the Answer Sheet with a
single line through the center.

Passage One

11. A. On the third Sunday in May.

    B. On the second Sunday in March.

    C. On the third Sunday in March.

    D. On the second Sunday in May.

12. A. In 1972.   B. In 1914.

    C. In 1872.   D. In 1944.

13. A. In 1911.   B. In 1914.

    C. In 1972.   D. In 1924.

Passage Two

14. A. In Greece.   B. In Italy.

     C. In Rome.   D. In USA.

15. A. In Summer.   B. In Winter.

     C. In Spring.   D. In Autumn.

16. A. On the last Sunday in May.

     B. On the second Sunday in May.

     C. On December 10.

     D. On December 8.

Passage Three

17. A. 1925.   B. 1932.

     C. 1944.   D. 1949.

18. A. In 1925.   B. In 1932.

     C. In 1944.   D. In 1949.

19. A. In 1925.   B. In 1932.

     C. In 1950.   D. In 1949.

20. A. On May 5.   B. On July 1.

     C. On April 4.   D. On October 1.

Secton C

Directions: *In this section, you will hear a passage of about 100 words three times. The passage is printed on your Answer Sheet with about 20 words missing. First you will hear the whole passage from the beginning to the end just to get a general idea of it. Then, in the second reading, you will hear a signal indicating the beginning of a pause after each sentence, sometimes two sentences or just part of a sentence. During the pause, you must write down the missing words you have just heard in the corresponding space on the Answer Sheet. There is also a different signal indicating the end of the pause. When you hear this signal, you must get ready for what comes next from the recording. You can check what you have written when the passage is read to you once again without the pauses.*

__(21)__ gap refers to a broad __(22)__ in values and __(23)__ between one generation and another, __(24)__ between young people and their __(25)__ . Why is there such a big gap between the children and parents? As we all __(26)__ , the __(27)__ has changed, so has the __(28)__ and that changes the __(29)__ of children. Today's generation doesn't like parents __(30)__ them, and if they try and tell them what's __(31)__ for them. And at __(32)__ , the society __(33)__ very __(34)__ and the parents can't __(35)__ up with new __(36)__ and __(37)__ , because they have __(38)__ to a __(39)__ lifestyle. So they find it __(40)__ to change it.

Part Three Reading Comprehension

Section A

Directions: *In this section, there is a passage with 10 blanks. You are required to select one word for each blank from a list of choices given in a word bank following the passage. Read the passage through carefully before making your choices. Each choice in the bank is identified by a letter. Please mark the corresponding letter for each item on Answer Sheet with a single line through the center.* **You may not use any of words in the bank more than once.**

Word Bank

A. full-time	C. more	E. earning	G. counterparts	I. dilemma
B. challenge	D. balance	F. called	H. take	J. equally

Nowadays, more and __(41)__ women go out of their home and find a job. They are __(42)__ working mothers. They earn as much money as their male __(43)__ . They are treated __(44)__ . But they are also facing the problems. Being a __(45)__ worker and businesswoman is a __(46)__ . They have to learn how to __(47)__ work and home. Some people say that a good mother stays home to __(48)__ care of her children. The other people believe that a good mother helps her family by __(49)__ money. It is really a __(50)__ for the mothers.

Section B

Directions: *There are 2 passages in this section. Each passage is followed by some ques-*

tions or unfinished statements. For each of them there are four choices marked A, B, C and D. You should decide on the best choice and mark the corresponding letter on Answer Sheet with a single line through the center.

Passage One

As the saying goes, women hold up half the sky. That is the case. Nowadays, a growing number of women have become millionaires or even billionaires. A new report shows that, there are nine women in the world's fifty richest people. The richest woman in the world is Rosalia Mera who made a great amount of money by establishing her own company in America.

But women also confront themselves with some difficulties. For example, they can feel pressures from the work and families. Many women complain that the stress on to-day's women is enormous because they have to be perfect in every aspect of their life — personal and professional — or they're considered a failure. The path of women to positions of power is still being blocked by men who fear women and operate on foolish stereotypes. Only a handful of women hold CEO positions at major companies. Only a quarter of elected politicians are women. No woman has ever been elected to run a nation in North America. It certainly isn't because they can't do the job. Pressure for women in the workplace is also enormous because they have to continually prove themselves to get the same respect as men. Many women also get paid less than their male counterparts for doing the same job.

And in the eye of ordinary people, if a woman doesn't have children, she's failed as a woman, even if she is CEO of a company. She has got to be beautiful, smart, tall, rich, successful at her job, married to the right guy. And people think women are inferior to men. And women's strength is weak and they are not smarter, abler than men.

Questions 51 to 55 are based on the passage

51. How many women are there in Top Fifty world's richest people?

    A. 9.   B. 10.   C. 11.   D. 12.

52. Where does the richest self-made woman come from?

    A. Austria.   B. America.

    C. Spain.   D. Britain.

53. Which is the following statement INCORRECT according to the article?

A. Women must try to be perfect.

B. Women's salary is lower than the men's.

C. No woman leader was elected as president in North America.

D. Two quarters of women are elected politicians.

54. According to the tradition, what is considered failure for the women?

A. Having no children.

B. Not earning as much money as men.

C. Not marrying to a good guy.

D. Not having strong power.

55. What does the text mainly talk about?

A. Women's role.

B. Women's responsibility.

C. Women's pressure.

D. Women's social position.

Passage Two

The Women's Liberation Movement is the social struggle which aims to eliminate forms of oppression based on gender (性别) and to gain for women equal economic and social status and rights as are enjoyed by men.

The Women's Liberation Movement may have developed in three stages:

Firstly, it began in Europe in the 18th century. It was somehow related to the Enlightenment in which some women writers emerged. In their works, they proposed the notion of women's emancipation(解放) for the first time. Secondly, by the late nineteenth century, a number of women were working in the professions and playing an active role in social life. This was called the second wave of Women's Liberation Movement. This was especially true in the colonies, where the gender imbalance in the population gave women greater power to promote their role. It was generally only after the First World War that Women's Suffrage was achieved, with 28 countries granting the vote to women between 1914 and 1939. In 1933, Sweden became the first country to make sex education for girls compulsory. In the Soviet Union, all women were promised equality in law and equal pay in 1918. Thirdly, the feminist movement developed quickly in the USA from 1960s to 1980s. In the early sixties feminism was still an unmentionable, but its ghost was slowly awakening from the dead. The first sign of new life came with the establishment of the Commission on the Status of Women by President Kennedy in 1961. Created at the urging of Esther Petersen of the Women's Bureau, in its short life the Commission came out with several often radical reports thoroughly documenting women's second class status. It was followed by the formation of a citizen's advisory council and fifty state commissions.

Many of the people involved in these commissions became the nucleus of women who, dissatisfied with the lack of progress made on commission recommendations, joined with Betty Friedan in 1966 to found the National Organization for Women.

Despite the failure of American campaigners to get the Equal Rights Amendment to the Constitution passed by enough states — the feminist movement has succeeded in changing the role of women and their public perception.

Questions 56 to 60 are based on the passage.

56. When did the Women's Liberation Movement first begin?

    A. In the 15th century.

    B. In the 16th century.

    C. In the 17th century.

    D. In the 18th century.

57. When did the second wave of Women's Liberation Movement begin?

    A. By the 17th century.

    B. In the 18th century.

    C. By the 19th century.

    D. By the 20th century.

58. Which country became the first to make education for girls compulsory?

    A. Sweden.　　　　　　　　　B. Russia.

    C. America.　　　　　　　　　D. Switzerland.

59. Who established the Commission on the Status of Women?

    A. President Roosevelt.

    B. President Kennedy.

    C. President Lincoln.

    D. President Kart.

60. When was the National Organization for Women formed?

    A. In 1961.　　　　　　　　　B. In 1962.

C. In 1966.   D. In 1964.

Part Four Vocabulary

Directions: *For this part you are required to choose the best answer from A, B, C and D to complete the following sentences.*

61. "What can you learn _____ your failure?" the teacher asked.

   A. from   B. at   C. on   D. /

62. Don't give _____, and keep doing it. You will be successful.

   A. in   B. out   C. off   D. up

63. The book is _____ with a lot of interesting stories.

   A. filled   B. fill   C. full   D. filling

64. My car broke down and I had it _____ right now.

   A. repair   B. repairing   C. repaired   D. to repair

65. When the movie star entered the room, the audience _____ into thunderous applause.

   A. burst   B. came   C. take   D. burnt

66. When he heard the news, he was shocked into _____ immediately.

   A. still   B. stillness   C. stilling   D. stilled

67. He said he had a lot of trouble _____ with different things in business.

   A. deal   B. to deal   C. dealing   D. to deal

68. He moved to a new place and felt _____ place

   A. out of   B. outside   C. in   D. inside

69. Neither she nor I _____ a student.

   A. is   B. am   C. are   D. were

70. He can speak English in addition _____ French.

   A. from   B. at   C. on   D. to

71. I was about to go to the filling station. The petrol was running _____.

   A. up   B. at   C. to   D. out

72. The market responded quickly _____ the government's regulations.

   A. to   B. at   C. in   D. /

73. What he said set everyone at present _____ guard.

   A. up   B. on   C. to   D. out

74. It seemed that the man was trying to _____ back his tears.

A. take   B. control

C. hold   D. get

75. We do believe that our team is _____ of winning the game.

A. capability   B. qualified

C. good   D. capable

76. He is in a _____ corner now, let's help him out of trouble.

A. difficult   B. close

C. hard   D. tight

77. The children are told to be _____ of the strangers.

A. cautious   B. warning

C. careless   D. mind

78. It is generally _____ that health is closely related to one's diet.

A. assuming   B. assume

C. assumed   D. to assume

79. He is frantic _____ that BMW car, but he can't afford it now.

A. for   B. on   C. at   D. of

80. The Prime Minister made a speech upon _____ at the airport.

A. arrive   B. got

C. arrival   D. to arrive

Part Five   Short Answer Questions

Directions: *In this part there is a short passage with five questions or incomplete state-ments. Read the passage carefully. Then answer the questions or complete the statement in the fewest possible words.*

Before 1949, there was a tradition in China, that is, the women's feet were bound when they were very young because the normal big feet were considered alien to feudal virtues.

When a girl turned about from three to six years old in China, her mother would use strips of cloth and start binding her feet. The wrappings would be taken off daily, then rewound tighter and tighter. Sometimes the toes would be broken right away and folded under the foot; otherwise they would just be gradually bound in that direction so they'd end up there. So the women's feet were three inches long. This 'ideal' length of a per-

65

fect foot was called the "Golden Lotus".

This practice traced back to the 9th century. One imperial concubine in Tang Dynasty began binding her feet because her husband loved little feet. Other women had to copy this practice. Since then on, women in China bound their feet and continued even when it was banned by the Manchuria who established the Qing Dynasty (1644-1911). Although the feet binding was officially abolished in 1949, in remote mountainous areas, women still had their feet bound even when the New China was founded in 1949.

The women with bound feet not only suffered from feet binding but also kept up with all daily duties including house cleaning and child raising. Nowadays, there are still some women whose feet were bound before 1949. One problem they are facing is that it is hard for them to buy the special shoes for bound feet on the market. Many shoe factories have stopped mass producing such kinds of "small shoes". They only make shoes on the basis of special order.

81. What is the tradition of foot binding?

82. How old did the girl begin binding their feet?

83. How did feet binding began becoming popular?

84. When did the feet binding put to an end officially?

85. What is the problem the women with bound feet are facing?

Part Six   Translation

Directions: *Finish the sentences on Answer Sheet by translating into English.*

86. 父母都不在家,我就可以独自享用电脑了。(have something to oneself)

87. 他在领悟新知识方面比我要快得多。(catch on)

88. 只要你下定决心做一件事情,你就一定会成功。(set one's mind to)

89. 很多问题阻碍了我们的成功,所以我们毫无选择,只能是一个一个的去解决它们。(stand in somebody's way)

90. 时间快到了,让我们在三分钟时间内把这件事情做完。(run out)

91. 他是班里前五名的学生,除此之外,他还乐于助人。(in addition)

92. 任何人都不能阻碍历史的发展。(hold back)

93. 当我走进屋子的时候,他瞥了我一眼,然后继续读他的小说。(go on)

94. 继续向前走,然后右转,你就能看到那家图书馆了。(go ahead)

95. 我们发现有必要帮助破产的公司摆脱财政危机。(help out)

Answer Sheet 1

Part One   Writing

_____
_____
_____
_____
_____
_____
_____
_____
_____
_____
_____
_____
_____
_____
_____
_____
_____
_____
_____
_____
_____

Part Two Listening Comprehension

Section C

   (21)   refers to a broad   (22)   in values and   (23)   between one generation and another,   (24)   between young people and their   (25) . Why is there a such big gap between the children and parents. As we all   (26) , the   (27)   has changed, so has the   (28)   and that changes the   (29)   of children. Today's generation doesn't like parents   (30)   them, and if they try and tell them what's   (31)   for them. And at   (32) , the society   (33)   very   (34)   and the parents can't   (35)   up with new   (36)   and   (37) , because they have   (38)   to a   (39)   lifestyle. So they find it   (40)   to change it.

Part Five Short Answer Questions

81. _____

_____

82. _____

_____

83. _____

_____

84. _____

_____

85. _____

_____

Part Six Translation

86. _____

_____

_____

_____

87. _____

_____

_____

88. _____

89.

90.

91.

92.

93.

94.

95.

Answer Sheet 2

Part Two   Listening Comprehension

Section A

1	2	3	4	5	6	7	8	9	10

Section B

11	12	13	14	15	16	17	18	19	20

Part Three   Reading Comprehension

Section A

41	42	43	44	45	46	47	48	49	50

Section B

51	52	53	54	55	56	57	58	59	60

Part Four   Vocabulary

61	62	63	64	65	66	67	68	69	70

71	72	73	74	75	76	77	78	79	80

Model Test 6

Part One Writing

Directions: *For this part, you are allowed 30 minutes to write a composition on the topic given in English. You should write at least 100 words.*

Innovation is the Key to Success

1. 当今,创新是一个国家、公司、个人生存和发展的首要条件;

2. 创新对于一个国家、公司、个人的成功的重要性;

3. 如何创新,呼吁社会要不断创新。

Part Two Listening Comprehension

Section A

Directions: *In this section you will hear 10 short conversations. At the end of each conversation, a question will be asked about what was said, both the conversation and the question will be spoken only once. After each question there will be a pause. During the pause, you must read the four choices marked A, B, C and D, and decide which is the best answer. Then mark the corresponding letter on the Answer sheet with a single line through the center.*

1. A. 1 million.   B. 2.5 million.

    C. 25 million.   D. 250 thousand.

2. A. Turn left.

    B. Continue walking.

    C. Turn right.

    D. Stay where he is.

3. A. 62040334.   B. 62030334.

C. 62040343.

D. 62040433.

4. A. On the desk.

B. Don't know.

C. At home.

D. Jack kept it.

5. A. At 11:30 am.

B. At 12:30 am.

C. At 12:00 am.

D. At 13:30 am.

6. A. Finance.

B. Civil engineering.

C. English.

D. Chemistry.

7. A. In the office.

B. At home.

C. In a restaurant.

D. At school.

8. A. Having a meeting.

B. Is free.

C. Meeting a client.

D. Staying at home.

9. A. This afternoon.

B. Tomorrow.

C. The day after tomorrow.

D. Tonight.

10. A. Mary.

B. Jack.

C. Tom's twin brother.

D. Tom.

Section B

Directions: *In this section, you will hear three short passages. At the end of each passage, you will hear some questions. Both the passage and the questions will be spoken only once. After you hear a question, you must choose the best answer from the four choices marked A, B, C and D, and decide which is the best answer. Then mark the corresponding letter on the Answer Sheet with a single line through the center.*

Passage One

11. A. In 1799.

B. In 1899.

C. In 1919.

D. In 1809.

12. A. Italy.

B. England.

C. France.

D. Germany.

13. A. In 1917.

B. In 1899.

C. In 1907.

D. In 1970.

Passage Two

14. A. In 1933. B. In 1943.
    C. In 1913. D. In 1923.

15. A. *The Old Man and the Sea*.
    B. *The Wrath of Grapes*.
    C. *A Farewell to Arms*.
    D. *For Whom the Bell Tolls*.

16. A. In 1923. B. In 1954.
    C. In 1944. D. In 1964.

Passage Three

17. A. Temperature. B. Heat.
    C. Distance. D. Speed.

18. A. 200. B. 100.
    C. 50. D. 80.

19. A. Celsius. B. Centigrade.
    C. Degree centigrade. D. Degree Celsius.

20. A. In 1948. B. In 1968.
    C. In 1958. D. In 1918.

Section C

Directions: *In this section, you will hear a passage of about 100 words three times. The passage is printed on your Answer Sheet with about 20 words missing. First you will hear the whole passage from the beginning to the end just to get a general idea of it. Then, in the second reading, you will hear a signal indicating the beginning of a pause after each sentence, sometimes two sentences or just part of a sentence. During the pause, you must write down the missing words you have just heard in the corresponding space on the Answer Sheet. There is also a different signal indicating the end of the pause. When you hear this signal, you must get ready for what comes next from the recording. You can check what you have written when the passage is read to you once again without the pauses.*

Two __(21)__ scales are in __(22)__ use in science and __(23)__. They are the degree __(24)__ (°C) scale, and the degree __(25)__. Celsius and Fahrenheit were both names of the __(26)__ of two scales. The __(27)__ was a Swedish __(28)__ and the latter came from __(29)__. Celsius and Fahrenheit __(30)__ their own temperature __(31)__ in __(32)__ and in 1724 __(33)__. Celsius took a __(34)__ thermometer, __(35)__ the __(36)__ point of water and the melting point of ice and marked it off into 100 __(37)__ degrees. In Fahrenheit's scale the __(38)__ point of ice 32° and the boiling point of water 212° are 180 degrees __(39)__. He also had a third point, the temperature of human's body which he __(40)__ was 98°.

Part Three   Reading Comprehension

Section A

Directions: *In this section, there is a passage with 10 blanks. You are required to select one word for each blank from a list of choices given in a word bank following the passage. Read the passage through carefully before making your choices. Each choice in the bank is identified by a letter. Please mark the corresponding letter for each item on Answer Sheet with a single line through the center.* **You may not use any of words in the bank more than once.**

Word Bank

A. freezing	C. called	E. symbol	G. proposed	I. primarily
B. capitalized	D. from	F. official	H. alone	J. exists

Apart __(41)__ the degree Celsius (°C) scale, and the degree Fahrenheit, there __(42)__ a third scale: the Kelvin (K) temperature scale. It is a temperature scale with the __(43)__ point of +273°K (Kelvin) and the boiling point of +373°K. It is used __(44)__ for scientific purposes. It was also known as the Absolute Temperature Scale. It was firstly __(45)__ in 1848 by William T. Kelvin, 1st Baron of Largs (1824-1907), Irish-born Scottish physicist and mathematician.

Temperatures on this scale are __(46)__ Kelvin, NOT degrees Kelvin, kelvin is not __(47)__, and the symbol (capital K) stands __(48)__ with no degree symbol. The __(49)__ name was changed to "kelvin" and __(50)__ "K" by the 13th General Conference on Weights and Measures (CGPM) in 1967.

Section B

Directions: *There are 2 passages in this section. Each passage is followed by some questions or unfinished statements. For each of them there are four choices marked A, B, C and D. You should decide on the best choice and mark the corresponding letter on Answer Sheet with a single line through the center.*

Passage One

Human beings are such curious creatures. The children are even more curious. When they were born, they are curious about everything new. And then they explore, question, and wonder. By pouring water into a dozen different-shaped bottles and on the floor and over clothes, the 4-year-old is learning pre-concepts of mass and volume. A child discovers the sweetness of candy, the bitterness of lemon, and the cold of ice.

The curious children are always trying something new. They are hungry to know about the world. They feed that hunger by exploring through their eyes, their ears, their mouths, their fingers. One interesting thing is that the children like repeating their behavior if they find one thing is very interesting because his discovery gives them pleasure. That is called the cycle of learning which is fueled by the curiosity. And at the same time, for the children, what is most pleasurable about discovery and mastery is sharing it with someone else. They are willing to share the joy and discovery with their friends or parents.

Parents play an important role in helping to sustain their children's curiosity. The teachers are next to the parents. The typical way to stimulate children's curiosity is to offer "science activities." Generally, though, early childhood educators offer an activity one day and move on to something quite different the next time. Yet, children's learning can be so much richer if we can offer them ways to keep on exploring the same phenomenon — with new materials or new tools.

Questions 51 to 55 are based on the passage.

51. According to the article, when will the human being begin to explore new things?

    A. At the age of 4.   B. At the age of 5.

    C. At the age of 3.   D. From the moment of birth.

52. When does a child know the concepts of mass and volume, according to the text?

    A. About 3 years old.　　　　　B. About 4 years old.

    C. About 5 years old.　　　　　D. About 6 years old.

53. What is the most pleasurable about discovery for a child?

    A. To find it by himself.

    B. To go to school.

    C. To share the joy with someone else.

    D. To discover something by repetition.

54. Who is playing a less important role in developing children's curiosity than their parents?

    A. Their Sister.　　　　　　　B. Their teacher.

    C. Their brother.　　　　　　　D. Their cousin.

55. What does the text mainly talk about?

    A. Children's curiosity.　　　　B. Children's interest.

    C. The role parents play.　　　　D. The role teachers play.

Passage Two

The Old Man and the Sea is one of Ernest Hemingway's most enduring works and may very well becomes one of the true classics of his times. It was published in 1952 to wide critical acclaim, it had been twelve years since his previous critical success, *For Whom the Bell Tolls*.

Although some critics say that the novel is full of the stilted language of some of the Spanish transliterations and the character Santiago's philosophizing is unrealistic, *The Old Man and the Sea* became an immediate success, selling 5.3 million copies within two days of its publication in a special edition of Life magazine. And one year later after it was published, the novel won the Pulitzer Prize for fiction. It also played a great part in his winning the 1954 Novel Prize for Literature and confirmed his power and presence in the literary world.

The Old Man and the Sea is generally considered by many to be his crowning achievement. The work was especially praised for its depiction of a new dimension to the typical Hemingway hero, less macho and more respectful of life. In Santiago, Hemingway had finally achieved a character who could face the human condition and survive without cynically dismissing it or dying while attempting to better it. In Santiago's relationship with the world and those around him, Hemingway had discovered a way to proclaim the power of love in a wider and deeper way than in his previous works.

Questions 56 to 60 are based on the passage.

56. When was Hemingway's work *For Whom the Bell Toll* published?

    A. In 1952.   B. In 1964.

    C. In 1942.   D. In 1940.

57. When did Hemingway win the Pulitzer Prize for fiction?

    A. In 1952.   B. In 1953.

    C. In 1954.   D. In 1955.

58. Which novel was considered as the highest achievement of Hemingway?

    A. *The Old Man and the Sea*.

    B. *For Whom the Bell Tolls*.

    C. *A Farewell to Arms*.

    D. *The Sun Also Rises*.

59. In what aspect did the critics thought *The Old Man and the Sea* was not a good novel?

    A. Depiction.   B. Characterization.

    C. Language.   D. Plot.

60. Which of the following is NOT true about the character Santiago?

    A. Masculine.   B. Be respectful of life.

    C. Try to live a better life.   D. Face the hard times.

Part Four Vocabulary

Directions: *For this part you are required to choose the best answer from A, B, C and D to complete the following sentences.*

61. The curious boy wants to know the difference _____ miles and kilograms.

    A. between   B. in   C. from   D. at

62. Recently a lot of people died _____ heart attack.

    A. from   B. between   C. of   D. on

63. Your face turns right, you'd better _____ to the doctor.

    A. going   B. go   C. to go   D. gone

64. When I entered the room, Mary stood there, _____ a book in her hand.

A. hold   B. to hold

C. holding   D. have hold

65. The doctor _____ my temperature and then prescribed some medicine for me.

A. took   B. got   C. made   D. put

66. My mother _____ her hand on my forehead and said I got a fever.

A. put   B. got   C. made   D. took

67. We were very worried about him because he was still _____ a critical condition.

A. on   B. at   C. in   D. off

68. You should avoid _____ vegetables that are grown with too many chemicals

A. eating   B. eat   C. to eat   D. eaten

69. Absent-minded, he seemed _____ from what the chairman was talking about

A. detach   B. detached

C. detaching   D. have detached

70. I would rather _____ at home than go outside for a walk.

A. staying   B. to stay

C. stay   D. have stayed

71. What a beautiful mountain! It is covered _____ snow.

A. /   B. in

C. into   D. with

72. As the saying goes, out of _____, out of mind.

A. sight   B. seeing

C. belief   D. watching

73. It is natural that he _____ so.

A. does   B. to do

C. should do   D. has done

74. He is fine, there is nothing to _____.

A. worry about   B. worry

C. worried   D. be worried

75. We should learn how to _____ ourselves from getting bored.

A. get   B. take   C. keep   D. obtain

76. Go _____ ahead at the traffic lights and then turn right

A. straightly   B. straight

C. straighten   D. straighter

77. Nowadays, more and more people realize that to keep healthy is of great _____.

    A. important

    B. being important

    C. importance

    D. to be important

78. I commenced _____ English at the age of 10.

    A. learning

    B. learn

    C. /

    D. having learned

79. The off springs of Confucius are _____ in many parts of China.

    A. scattering

    B. to scatter

    C. scattered

    D. spreading

80. The teacher were _____ his students how to do the exercises.

    A. destructing

    B. obstructing

    C. conducting

    D. instructing

Part Five   Short Answer Questions

Directions: *In this part there is a short passage with five questions or incomplete state-ments. Read the passage carefully. Then answer the questions or complete the statement in the fewest possible words.*

Thomas Edison was born to Sam and Nancy on February 11, 1847, in Milan, Ohio. When Edison was seven, his family moved to Port Huron, Michigan. Known as "Al" in his youth, Edison was the youngest of seven children, four of whom survived to adult-hood. Edison tended to be in poor health when young. What is worse is that around the age of twelve, Edison lost almost all his hearing.

Thomas Edison was not a good student. So he quitted the school and his mother taught him at home. At thirteen he took a job as a newsboy, selling newspapers and can-dy on the local railroad that ran through Port Huron to Detroit. Then at thirteen he took a job as a newsboy, selling newspapers and candy on the local railroad that ran through Port Huron to Detroit.

Later he became the greatest inventors in the USA. He made great contribution to human being by inventing lots of things. The first great invention developed by Edison was the tin foil phonograph. August 12, 1877, is the date popularly given for Edison's completion of the model for the first phonograph. Thomas Edison's greatest challenge was the development of a practical incandescent, electric light.

There are also plenty of sayings by Thomas Edison: Genius is one per cent inspiration and ninety-nine percent perspiration. I never did anything by accident, nor did any of my inventions come by accident; they came by work. Many of life's failures are people who did not realize how close they were to success when they gave up.

Until now, Thomas Edison was still well remembered as the one of the greatest scientists, inventors in the world.

81. At the age of seven, Thomas Edison's family moved from _____ to _____.

82. What was Edison's first job?

83. In which year did Edison almost lose his hearing?

84. What was his first invention and when did Edison finish it?

85. How to understand the saying: Genius is one per cent inspiration and ninety-nine percent perspiration?

Part Six   Translation

Directions: *Finish the sentences on Answer Sheet by translating into English*.

86. 政府已经采取很多措施降低城市中心的噪声污染。(bring down)

87. 从那以后,他开始对社交和感情都变得很冷漠。(be detached from)

88. 他宁可死也不愿向敌人投降。(would rather)

89. 我一直看着他走出门外,直到他消失。(out of sight)

90. 少数民族正在努力阻止他们文化的消亡。(keep from)

91. 放松,一切都会好的! (take it easy)

92. 凯瑟琳非常害怕以至于她不得不控制住自己不要大喊出来。(hold tight onto oneself)

93. 我为你开点药,记住每天服用三次。(prescribe)

94. 他在冰上滑了一跤,然后摔倒了。(slide)

95. 酸雨对土壤的腐蚀性很大。(acid)

Answer Sheet 1

Part One   Writing

Part Two Listening Comprehension

Section C

Two __(21)__ scales are in __(22)__ use in science and __(23)__ . They are the degree __(24)__ (°C) scale, and the degree __(25)__ . Celsius and Fahrenheit were both names of the __(26)__ of two scales. The __(27)__ was a Swedish __(28)__ and the latter came from __(29)__ . Celsius and Fahrenheit __(30)__ their own temperature __(31)__ in __(32)__ and in 1724 __(33)__ . Celsius took a __(34)__ thermometer, __(35)__ the __(36)__ point of water and the melting point of ice and marked it off into 100 __(37)__ degrees. In Fahrenheit's scale the __(38)__ point of ice 32° and the boiling point of water 212° are 180 degrees __(39)__ . He also had a third point, the temperature of human's body which he __(40)__ was 98°.

Part Five Short Answer Questions

81. _____

_____

82. _____

_____

83. _____

_____

84. _____

_____

85. _____

_____

Part Six Translation

86. _____

_____

_____

87. _____

_____

_____

88. _____
_____
_____

89. _____
_____
_____

90. _____
_____
_____

91. _____
_____
_____

92. _____
_____
_____

93. _____
_____
_____

94. _____
_____
_____

95. _____
_____
_____

Answer Sheet 2

Part Two Listening Comprehension

Section A

1	2	3	4	5	6	7	8	9	10

Section B

11	12	13	14	15	16	17	18	19	20

Part Three Reading Comprehension

Section A

41	42	43	44	45	46	47	48	49	50

Section B

51	52	53	54	55	56	57	58	59	60

Part Four Vocabulary

61	62	63	64	65	66	67	68	69	70

71	72	73	74	75	76	77	78	79	80

Model Test 7

Part One Writing

Directions: *For this part, you are allowed 30 minutes to write a composition on the topic given in English. You should write at least 100 words.*

My Attitude towards War

1. 全球各地还存在着局部战争,而且有升级的可能;

2. 战争爆发的原因,以及你对战争的看法;

3. 呼吁全球各国联合起来防止战争的爆发。

Part Two Listening Comprehension

Section A

Directions: *In this section you will hear 10 short conversations. At the end of each conversation, a question will be asked about what was said, both the conversation and the question will be spoken only once. After each question there will be a pause. During the pause, you must read the four choices marked A, B, C and D, and decide which is the best answer. Then mark the corresponding letter on the Answer Sheet with a single line through the center.*

1. A. Go to theatre.   B. Meet her friends.
   C. Go home.   D. Go back to her dorm.
2. A. They both have finished their papers.
   B. They both haven't finished their papers.
   C. Michael has finished his paper.
   D. Jane has finished her paper.
3. A. 40.   B. 50.   C. 15.   D. 10.
4. A. Banana.   B. Watermelon.

C. Plum. D. Pineapple.

5. A. 2. B. 5. C. 1. D. 3.

6. A. The man answered the second question.

B. The man didn't answer the first question.

C. The man answered the fourth question.

D. The man didn't answer the second question.

7. A. The Summer Palace.

B. The Forbidden City.

C. The Great Wall.

D. Tiananmen Square.

8. A. $ 20. B. $ 30. C. $ 10. D. $ 40.

9. A. 1753. B. 1375. C. 1735. D. 1573.

10. A. English. B. Law.

C. Chinese. D. French.

Section B

Directions: *In this section, you will hear three short passages. At the end of each passage, you will hear some questions. Both the passage and the questions will be spoken only once. After you hear a question, you must choose the best answer from the four choices marked A, B, C and D, and decide which is the best answer. Then mark the corresponding letter on the Answer Sheet with a single line through the center.*

Passage One

11. A. Latin. B. Greek.

C. French. D. German.

12. A. Radio. B. Film.

C. An open area. D. Theatre.

13. A. Music. B. Action.

C. Opera. D. Musical.

Passage Two

14. A. In the late 19th century.

B. In the early 19th century.

C. In the late 18th century.

D. In the early 18th century.

15. A. In the mid-19th century.

B. In the early 19th century.

C. In the late 19th century.

D. In the late 18th century.

16. A. Anhui Province.

B. Beijing.

C. Hebei Province.

D. Hunan Province.

Passage Three

17. A. Ancient Egypt.   B. Ancient China.

C. Ancient Rome.   D. Ancient Greece.

18. A. 1.   B. 2.   C. 3.   D. 4.

19. A. Twice a year.   B. Once a year.

C. Once two years.   D. Once three years.

20. A. Tragedy.   B. Comedy.

C. Satire.   D. Opera.

Section C

Directions: *In this section, you will hear a passage of about 100 words three times. The passage is printed on your Answer Sheet with about 20 words missing. First you will hear the whole passage from the beginning to the end just to get a general idea of it. Then, in the second reading, you will hear a signal indicating the beginning of a pause after each sentence, sometimes two sentences or just part of a sentence. During the pause, you must write down the missing words you have just heard in the corresponding space on the Answer Sheet. There is also a different signal indicating the end of the pause. When you hear this signal, you must get ready for what comes next from the recording. You can check what you have written when the passage is read to you once again without the pauses.*

Western opera is a ___(21)___ art form, which arose during the ___(22)___ in an attempt to revive the classical ___(23)___ drama tradition. Both music and ___(24)___ were combined in the Greek Drama. Due to the ___(25)___ with western ___(26)___ music, great ___(27)___ have taken place in ___(28)___ in the past four hundred years and it is an important ___(29)___ of theatre until this day. The ___(30)___ 19th century composer Richard Wagner exerted enormous ___(31)___ on the opera tradition. In his ___(32)___, there was no proper ___(33)___ between music and theatre in the operas of his time, because the music seemed to be more ___(34)___ than the dramatic ___(35)___ in these works. To restore the connection with the ___(36)___ Greek drama, he ___(37)___ renewed the operatic format, and to ___(38)___ the equally importance of music and ___(39)___ in these new works, he ___(40)___ them "music dramas".

Part Three   Reading Comprehension

Section A

Directions: *In this section, there is a passage with 10 blanks. You are required to select one word for each blank from a list of choices given in a word bank following the passage. Read the passage through carefully before making your choices. Each choice in the bank is identified by a letter. Please mark the corresponding letter for each item on Answer Sheet with a single line through the center.* **You may not use any of words in the bank more than once.**

Word Bank

A. more	C. back	E. formed	G. explosion	I. started
B. permanent	D. characterized	F. issue	H. attacks	J. available

U.S. civil defense goes ___(41)___ to ancient times, when fortified city-states came under siege (包围), including crude biological ___(42)___. However, civil defense became a major ___(43)___ during World War I because the factories and other place would be attacked by the enemies. Civil defense became even ___(44)___ important during World War II.

The ___(45)___ of the Soviet Union's first atomic, and then hydrogen(氢), bombs signaled the fact that civil defense would remain a ___(46)___ fixture of the Cold War.

In response to the Soviet's first atomic explosion and the Korean War, the Federal Civil Defense Administration was ___(47)___ in 1951.

During the 1950s, American civil defense was ___(48)___ by a city-evacuation system. Because long-range bombers were the only means ___(49)___ to deliver nuclear devices, it was assumed that several hours of warning would precede an attack. Both Germany and Britain had used evacuation, or crisis relocation, with mixed results, during World War II.

The American Civil Defense Association was ___(50)___ in the early 1960's in response to its nations reliance on atomic weaponry as a centerpiece of foreign policy following World War II, up to and including the onset of the Cold War.

With the help of the civil defense program, civilian may easily escape from the dangers or attacks.

Section B

Directions: *There are 2 passages in this section. Each passage is followed by some questions or unfinished statements. For each of them there are four choices marked A, B, C and D. You should decide on the best choice and mark the corresponding letter on Answer Sheet with a single line through the center.*

Passage One

A National Missile Defense (NMD) system has been the topic of much debate in the United States for more than half a century. According to its supporters, such a system would provide a sort of protective shield against a limited missile attack. In 1999, the U. S. Congress decided that the time for talk was over — they passed a bill calling for the implementation of the NMD system to defend the United States from a growing number of countries developing long-range missile technologies.

U. S. National Missile Defense (NMD) as a generic term(专业术语) is a military strategy and associated systems to shield an entire country against incoming Intercontinental Ballistic Missiles (ICBMs)(洲际导弹). The missiles could be intercepted by other missiles, or possibly by lasers. They could be intercepted near the launch point (boost phase), during flight through space (mid-course phase), or during atmospheric descent (terminal phase).

The objective of the National Missile Defense (NMD) program is to develop and maintain the option to deploy a cost effective, operationally effective, and Anti-Ballistic Missile (ABM)(反弹道导弹) Treaty compliant system that will protect the United States against limited ballistic missile threats, including accidental or unauthorized launches or Third World threats.

The primary mission of National Missile Defense is defense of the United States (all 50 states) against a threat of a limited strategic ballistic missile attack from a rogue nation. Such a system would also provide some capability against a small accidental or unauthorized launch of strategic ballistic missiles from more nuclear capable states.

The National Missile Defense Program was originally a technology development effort. In 1996, at the direction of the Secretary of Defense, NMD was designated a Major Defense Acquisition Program and transitioned to an acquisition effort. Concurrently, BMDO was tasked with developing a deployable system within three years. This three-year development period culminated in 2000, and the Department of Defense began a Deployment Readiness Review in June 2000. Using that review, President Clinton was to make a deployment decision based on four criteria: the potential ICBM threat to the United States; the technical readiness of the NMD system; the projected cost of the NMD system; and potential environmental impact of the NMD system. Rather than make a decision, President Clinton deferred the deployment decision to his successor. The White House in choosing this action cited several factors. Among them were the lack of test under realistic conditions, the absence of testing of the booster rocket, and lingering questions over the system's ability to deal with countermeasures. The deployment decision now rests with President George W. Bush, who is reexamining the Clinton NMD system along with a variety of other proposals. In the meantime, work is continuing on technology development for the NMD system.

Questions 51 to 55 are based on the passage.

51. What does the National Missile Defense (NMD) system provide a shield against?

    A. Missile Attacks.   B. Terrorist Attacks.

    C. Domestic crimes.   D. foreign countries.

52. What is the major mission of NMD?

    A. To deploy an effective system.

    B. To intercept the Intercontinental Ballistic Missiles.

    C. To defend the United States.

D. To intercept long-range missiles.

53. What was the origin of NMD?

   A. A technological development program.

   B. Defense of national security.

   C. Development of nuclear weapons.

   D. The plan to strengthen national power.

54. When did the development of deployable system reach its peak?

   A. In 1998.   B. In 1999.

   C. In 2000.   D. In 2001.

55. Based on how many criteria did President Clinton make a deployment decision?

   A. 1.   B. 2.   C. 3.   D. 4.

Passage Two

Prior to 1951, there was no method that the U. S government could use to broadcast warnings to citizens in the event of an emergency. However, radio stations and networks could interrupt normal programming and issue a bulletin in the event of an emergency, as what happened during the attack on Pearl Harbor on December 7, 1941, as well as the first successful tornado warning near Tinker Air Force Base in Oklahoma City in 1948. This type of broadcasting was the forerunner to CONELRAD.

In 1951, President Harry S. Truman signed legislation authorizing CONELRAD to begin operation. Conelrad (CONtrol of ELectronic RADiation) was set up in 1951 to provide warnings to the public during the Cold War.

CONELRAD had a simple system for alerting the public and other "downstream" stations that consisted of a sequence of shutting the station off for five seconds, returning to the air for five seconds, again shutting down for five seconds, and then transmitting a tone for 15 seconds. Key stations would be alerted directly. All other broadcast stations would monitor a designated station in an area. In the event of an emergency, all United States television and FM radio stations were required to stop broadcasting. Upon alert, most Mediumwave stations shut down. The stations that stayed on the air would transmit on either 640 or 1240 kHz. They would transmit for several minutes, and then go off the air and another station would take over on the same frequency in a "round robin" chain. This was to confuse enemy aircraft who might be navigating using Radio Direction Finding. By law, radio sets manufactured between 1953 and 1963 had these frequencies marked by the triangle-in-circle (CD Mark) symbol of Civil Defense.

CONELRAD required all AM stations in the United States to **sign off** in the event of an enemy attack, save for those designated to stay on the air at either 640 or 1240. Multiple signals on the same frequency, coming from different directions, would prevent enemy planes from using one station as a direction finder.

Questions 56 to 60 are based on the passage.

56. When did CONELRAD begin its operation?

    A. In 1952.   B. In 1953.

    C. In 1963.   D. In 1951.

57. When did Japanese troops attack Pearl Harbor?

    A. On December 13, 1941.

    B. On December 7, 1941.

    C. On November 7, 1943.

    D. On December 8, 1941.

58. Upon alert, which of the following frequency did all stations move to?

    A. 1024kHz.   B. 630kHz.

    C. 1000kHz.   D. 1020kHz.

59. What does the phrase "sign off" mean in the last Para. ?

    A. Disappear.   B. Help government.

    C. Stop broadcasting.   D. Appear.

60. What does the text mainly talk about?

    A. CONELRAD and its function.

    B. CONELRAD.

    C. History of CONELRAD.

    D. Introduction of CONELRAD.

Part Four   Vocabulary

Directions: *For this part you are required to choose the best answer from A , B , C and D to complete the following sentences.*

61. In this movie, the man was killed _____ a stormy evening.

    A. in   B. on   C. at   D. with

62. An announcement came _____ the radio that everyone should stay at home in the

event of war.

    A. /   B. off   C. over   D. with

63. _____ the midist of the Second Industrial Revolution, it was a generation who focused on building the future.

    A. At   B. With   C. On   D. In

64. A good friend is not the one who breaks _____ the friendship when you are in trouble.

    A. up   B. off   C. down   D. out

65. Fortunately, the family _____ the big fire last night.

    A. survived at   B. was surviving C. survived   D. survived in

66. He immediately signed the contract _____ the simple reason that he could make a big profit.

    A. for   B. in   C. with   D. on

67. He was told to grab _____ of the rope and then he would be lifted out of the hole.

    A. /   B. get   C. hold   D. holding

68. The laptop computer is a _____ computer that you can take to any place you want.

    A. port   B. ported

    C. porter   D. portable

69. The police told the local residents that we were still _____ a state of Red Alert.

    A. in   B. at

    C. under   D. on

70. Let's _____ lots to decide who will cook the meal tonight.

    A. get   B. take

    C. draw   D. obtain

71. It was not the time that the school _____ books to the students.

    A. supplies   B. is supplying

    C. was supplied   D. supplied

72. I tell him that he should keep _____ so and will soon be successful.

    A. do   B. to do

    C. doing   D. done

73. The members pleaded _____ the chairman that their proposal would be passed.

    A. with   B. at   C. /   D. on

74. The clothes _____ a great deal of differences, he looked much younger now.

    A. kept   B. had   C. made   D. took

75. Looking at the snake approaching him, Jack's face _____ white.

    A. went   B. took   C. took on   D. went in

76. The sight of a lake at the _____ of the ocean is amazing.

    A. floor   B. ground   C. bottom   D. end

77. They are trying to figure _____ what's wrong with their computer.

    A. out   B. on

    C. off   D. at

78. Seeing him fall off the bike, I walked to him, helping him _____ his feet.

    A. in   B. on   C. up   D. out of

79. The siren sounds were still _____ in my ears.

    A. echoing   B. getting

    C. ringing   D. surrounding

80. After his mother's death, his grief was really _____ words.

    A. out of   B. off

    C. in no   D. beyond

Part Five Short Answer Questions

Directions: *In this part there is a short passage with five questions or incomplete state-ments. Read the passage carefully. Then answer the questions or complete the statement in the fewest possible words.*

World War II was the mightiest struggle humankind has ever seen. It killed more people, cost more money, damaged more property, affected more people, and caused more far-reaching changes in nearly every country than any other war in history. The number of people killed, wounded, or missing between September 1939 and September 1945 can never be calculated, but it is estimated that more than 55 million people per-ished. More than 50 countries took part in the war, and the whole world felt its effects. What are the causes of the war?

Many historians trace the roots of World War II to the Treaty of Versailles and other peace agreements that followed World War I. The Germans found it easy to blame the harsh Treaty of Versailles for their troubles.

Germany set up a republican form of government in 1919. Many Germans blamed

94

the new government for accepting the hated treaty. People who could not find jobs began to drift into the Communist and National Socialist parties. As the government lost power, Adolf Hitler and his National Socialist or Nazi party grew stronger.

When the stock market crashed on October 29, 1929, the financial crisis had worldwide consequences and the reaction of nations to the dire financial straits of the Depression had a huge impact.

Economic problems were among the fundamental causes of World War II. Germany, Italy, and Japan considered themselves unjustly handicapped in trying to compete with other nations for markets, raw materials, and colonies. They believed that such countries as Belgium, France, Great Britain, the Netherlands, and the United States unfairly controlled most of the world's wealth and people. So, Germany, Italy, and Japan began to look for lands to conquer in order to obtain what they considered to be their share of the world's resources and markets.

The Depression destroyed the market for imported silk from Japan, which had provided the country with two-fifths of its export income. Military leaders took control of the government, and in 1931, Japan invaded China, looking for more raw materials and bigger markets for her factories.

The League of Nations called a conference of 60 nations in Geneva, Switzerland, in 1932. The conference was one in a long line of disarmament conferences that had been occurring since the end of World War I.

Germany, whose military power had been severely limited by the Treaty of Versailles, announced that world disarmament had to be accomplished, or Germany would rearm and achieve military equality. France refused to disarm until an international police system could be established.

The conference adjourned temporarily and by the time it was back in session, Hitler had become chancellor of Germany and was already preparing to rearm. Germany withdrew from the conference, which ended in failure, without any hope for disarmament.

81. How many people died in the WWII according to the article?

82. According to many histories, what are the roots of WWII?

83. The World War II started in _____, and ended in _____.

84. Which three countries launched the world war to conquer the world?

85. What are the reasons for the World War II the author lists in the article?

Part Six   Translation

Directions: *Finish the sentences on Answer Sheet by translating into English.*

86. 这个屋子太小,不能同时放置两张桌子。(fit in)

87. 上周末我们去海边看日出了。(come up)

88. 看完比赛之后,我们去了酒吧。(head for)

89. 那些说话算数的女性往往比她们的男性同行干得出色。(mean business)

90. 到了月底总是要积压大量的工作。(pile up)

91. 今天下午我很累,但是我实在不应该那样大发脾气。(blow one's top)

92. 我妹妹三天前开始从事教学工作。(take up)

93. 由于天气原因,我们不得不取消了我们的这次旅行。(call off)

94. 他考试没及格,我看不起他,因为他从来都没有努力使自己及格。(hold...against)

95. 她不懂人情世故。(in the way of)

Answer Sheet 1

Part One Writing

_____

_____

_____

_____

_____

_____

_____

_____

_____

_____

_____

_____

_____

_____

_____

_____

_____

_____

_____

_____

_____

Part Two Listening Comprehension

Section C

Western opera is a __(21)__ art form, which arose during the __(22)__ in an attempt to revive the classical __(23)__ drama tradition. Both music and __(24)__ were combined in the Greek Drama. Due to the __(25)__ with western __(26)__ music, great __(27)__ have taken place in __(28)__ in the past four hundred years and it is an important __(29)__ of theatre until this day. The __(30)__ 19th century composer Richard Wagner exerted enormous __(31)__ on the opera tradition. In his __(32)__ , there was no proper __(33)__ between music and theatre in the operas of his time, because the music seemed to be more __(34)__ than the dramatic __(35)__ in these works. To restore the connection with the __(36)__ Greek drama, he __(37)__ renewed the operatic format, and to __(38)__ the equally importance of music and __(39)__ in these new works, he __(40)__ them "music dramas".

Part Five Short Answer Questions

81. _____

_____

82. _____

_____

83. _____

_____

84. _____

_____

85. _____

_____

Part Six Translation

86. _____

_____

_____

87. _____

88.

89.

90.

91.

92.

93.

94.

95.

Answer Sheet 2

Part Two Listening Comprehension

Section A

1	2	3	4	5	6	7	8	9	10

Section B

11	12	13	14	15	16	17	18	19	20

Part Three Reading Comprehension

Section A

41	42	43	44	45	46	47	48	49	50

Section B

51	52	53	54	55	56	57	58	59	60

Part Four Vocabulary

61	62	63	64	65	66	67	68	69	70

71	72	73	74	75	76	77	78	79	80

Model Test 8

Part One　Writing

Directions: *For this part, you are allowed 30 minutes to write a composition on the topic given in English. You should write at least 100 words.*

The Importance of Keeping Fit Mentally

1. 现代社会,人们在保持身体健康的同时,开始关注心理健康;
2. 保持心理健康的重要性;
3. 如何保持心理健康。

Part Two　Listening Comprehension

Section A

Directions: *In this section you will hear 10 short conversations. At the end of each conversation, a question will be asked about what was said, both the conversation and the question will be spoken only once. After each question there will be a pause. During the pause, you must read the four choices marked A, B, C and D, and decide which is the best answer. Then mark the corresponding letter on the Answer sheet with a single line through the center.*

1. A. Cloudy.　　　　　　　　　B. Sunny.
   C. Drizzly.　　　　　　　　　D. Overcast.
2. A. In America.　　　　　　　　B. In France.
   C. In China.　　　　　　　　　D. In Australia.
3. A. 2 hours.　　　　　　　　　B. 1 hour.
   C. 3 hours.　　　　　　　　　D. 4 hours.
4. A. Good.　　　　　　　　　　B. So-so.
   C. Surprising.　　　　　　　　D. Boring.

5. A. 5:55.   B. 5:56.

     C. 5:50.   D. 6:00.

6. A. The supermarket.   B. The KFC.

     C. The bank.   D. The bookstore.

7. A. Japanese.   B. English.

     C. Germany.   D. French.

8. A. A lot of cars on the road.

     B. Running out of petrol.

     C. Bad weather.

     D. The careless driver.

9. A. In 2005.   B. In 2006.

     C. In 2007.   D. In 2008.

10. A. 1 year.   B. 2 years.

     C. 3 years.   D. 4 years.

Section B

Directions: *In this section, you will hear three short passages. At the end of each passage, you will hear some questions. Both the passage and the questions will be spoken only once. After you hear a question, you must choose the best answer from the four choices marked A, B, C and D, and decide which is the best answer. Then mark the corresponding letter on the Answer Sheet with a single line through the center.*

Passage One

11. A. Tiredness.   B. Laziness.

     C. Happiness.   D. Laughter.

12. A. In the late 1900s.

     B. In the late 1880s.

     C. In the late 1700s.

     D. In the late 1800s.

13. A. To daydream everyday.

     B. To let their parents daydream.

     C. To daydream once a week.

D. To let their children daydream.

Passage Two

14. A. In the late 1860s. B. In the late 1960s.
    C. In the late 1760s. D. In the late 1970s.

15. A. Yale University.

    B. The City College of New York.

    C. New York University.

    D. State University of New York.

16. A. 3. B. 4. C. 5. D. 6.

Passage Three

17. A. In 1984. B. In 1874.
    C. In 1974. D. In 1774.

18. A. 1. B. 2. C. 3. D. 4.

19. A. Their mind wanders. B. Unpleasant emotions.
    C. Fears of failure. D. Self-doubt.

20. A. Anxiety. B. Aggression.
    C. Hostility. D. Pleasant daydreams.

Section C

Directions: *In this section, you will hear a passage of about 100 words three times. The passage is printed on your Answer Sheet with about 20 words missing. First you will hear the whole passage from the beginning to the end just to get a general idea of it. Then, in the second reading, you will hear a signal indicating the beginning of a pause after each sentence, sometimes two sentences or just part of a sentence. During the pause, you must write down the missing words you have just heard in the corresponding space on the Answer Sheet. There is also a different signal indicating the end of the pause. When you hear this signal, you must get ready for what comes next from the recording. You can check what you have written when the passage is read to you once again without the pauses.*

Sigmund Freud, an ___(21)___ physician was born on May 6, ___(22)___ . He ___(23)___ the ___(24)___ of psychology. Freud is best ___(25)___ for his ___(26)___ of the unconscious mind. He ___(27)___ his theory through a ___(28)___ form of dialogue between a ___(29)___ and a psychoanalyst. He is also ___(30)___ for his redefinition of sexual ___(31)___ as the primary motivational ___(32)___ of human life. It is ___(33)___ toward a wide variety of ___(34)___ , as well as his unique ___(35)___ , including the use of ___(36)___ association, and the interpretation of ___(37)___ as sources of ___(38)___ into unconscious desires. He ___(39)___ away on ___(40)___ 23, 1939.

Part Three   Reading Comprehension

Section A

Directions: *In this section, there is a passage with 10 blanks. You are required to select one word for each blank from a list of choices given in a word bank following the passage. Read the passage through carefully before making your choices. Each choice in the bank is identified by a letter. Please mark the corresponding letter for each item on Answer Sheet with a single line through the center.* **You may not use any of words in the bank more than once.**

Word Bank

A. including	C. detail	E. respects	G. debate	I. original
B. frequently	D. variety	F. to	H. generally	J. influential

Sigmund Freud, medical doctor, psychologist and father of psychoanalysis, is ___(41)___ recognized as one of the most ___(42)___ thinkers of the twentieth century. Freud explained in ___(43)___ the theory that the mind is a complex energy-system. In spite of the multiple manifestations of psychoanalysis as it exists today, it can in almost all fundamental ___(44)___ be traced directly back to Freud's ___(45)___ work. Further, Freud's innovative treatment of human actions, dreams, etc. has proven to be extraordinarily productive, and has had massive implications for a wide ___(46)___ of fields, ___(47)___ anthropology, semiotics, and artistic creativity and appreciation in addition ___(48)___ psychology. However, Freud's most important and ___(49)___ repeated claim, that with psychoanalysis he had invented a new science of the mind, remains the subject of much critical ___(50)___ and controversy.

104

Section B

Directions: *There are 2 passages in this section. Each passage is followed by some questions or unfinished statements. For each of them there are four choices marked A, B, C and D. You should decide on the best choice and mark the corresponding letter on Answer Sheet with a single line through the center.*

Passage One

Florence Nightingale was born on 12 May 1820, and named after the city of her birth. Her wealthy parents were in Florence as part of a tour of Europe. In 1837, she began to develop an interest in nursing, but her parents continued it to be a profession inappropriate to a woman of her class and background, and would not allow her to train as a nurse.

Inspired by what she took as a Christian divine calling, experienced first in 1837 at Embley Park and later throughout Florence's life, she committed herself to nursing (though discouraged by her parents). This demonstrated a passion on her part, and also a rebellion against the expected role for a woman of her status, which was to become a wife and mother. In those days, nursing was a career with a poor reputation, filled mostly by poorer women, "hangers-on" who followed the armies. In fact, nurses were equally likely to function as cooks. Nightingale announced her decision to enter nursing in 1845 bringing intense anger and distress to her family, particularly her mother.

Nightingale's parents eventually relented and in 1851, she went to Kaiserwerth in Germany for three months nursing training. This enabled her to become superintendent of a hospital for gentlewomen in Harley Street, in 1853. The following year, the Crimean War began and soon reports in the newspapers were describing the desperate lack of proper medical facilities for wounded British soldiers at the front. Sidney Herbert, the war minister, already knew Nightingale, and asked her to oversee a team of nurses in the military hospitals in Turkey. In November 1854, she arrived in Scutari in Turkey. With her nurses, she greatly improved the conditions and substantially reduced the mortality rate.

She returned to England in 1856. In 1860 she established the Nightingale Training School for nurses at St Thomas' Hospital in London. Once the nurses were trained, they were sent to hospitals all over Britain, where they introduced the ideas they had learnt, and established nursing training on the Nightingale model. Nightingale's theories, published in 'Notes on Nursing' (1860), were hugely influential and her concerns for sanitation, military health and hospital planning established practices which are still in existence today. She died on 13 August 1910.

Questions 51 to 55 are based on the passage.

51. Where was Nightingale born?

    A. In Germany.   B. In England.

    C. In Turkey.   D. In Italy.

52. When did Nightingale show her interesting in nursing?

    A. At the age of17.   B. At the age of 18 .

    C. At the age of 25   D. At the age of 26.

53. When did Florence Nightingale enter nursing?

    A. In 1837.   B. In 1853.

    C. In 1845.   D. In 1854.

54. What did Nightingale's parents react to her decision to become a nurse at the beginning?

    A. Be angry.   B. Totally agree.

    C. Be happy.   D. Support.

55. What does this passage mainly talk about?

    A. Nightingale's work.   B. Nightingale and her nursing work.

    C. Nightingale and her family.   D. Nightingale and her life.

Passage Two

The Nightingale Award or The Nightingale Medal, established at the Ninth International Red Cross Conference in Washington in 1912, is presented by International Committee of the Red Cross. Conferment takes place every two years on May 12, Florence Nightingale's birthday.

It is an award special for qualified male or female nurses and also for male or female voluntary nursing aides who are active members or regular helpers of a National Red Cross or Red Crescent Society or of an affiliated medical or nursing institution. The award aims at honoring those persons who have distinguished themselves in times of peace or war by exceptional courage and devotion to the wounded, sick or disabled or to civilian victims of a conflict or disaster, and exemplary services or a creative and pioneering spirit in the areas of public health or nursing education. The Medal may be awarded ***posthumously*** if the prospective recipient has fallen on active service.

Questions 55 to 60 are based on the passage.

56. When was the Nightingale Award established?

    A. In 1914.   B. In 1913.

    C. In 1923.   D. In 1912.

57. Why was the Nightingale Award conferred on May 12?

    A. Because it is a special day for International Committee of the Red Cross.

    B. Because it is the birthday of Nightingale.

    C. The reason is not clear.

    D. Above of all.

58. How often is the Nightingale Award conferred?

    A. Twice one year.   B. Twice three years.

    C. Once two years.   D. Once a year.

59. Whom is the Nightingale Award established for?

    A. The teacher.   B. The soldier.

    C. The nurse.   D. The doctor.

60. What does the word ***posthumously*** mean in the last Paragraph?

    A. After death.   B. Honorably.

    C. Prospectively.   D. Actively.

Part Four   Vocabulary

Directions: *For this part you are required to choose the best answer from A, B, C and D to complete the following sentences.*

61. Students should be taught how to _____ their goals at school.

    A. get to   B. take   C. aimat   D. achieve

62. What you said at the meeting amounted _____ a proposal.

    A. up   B. at   C. to   D. with

63. "What is your attitude _____ globalization?" The man asked.

    A. attitude   B. on   C. at   D. about

64. Most of the students view speaking _____ the best way to learn English.

A. with   B. at   C. in   D. as

65. We have to wait, I think, it is _____ matter of time.

A. the   B. /   C. an   D. a

66. The historians deal with the same event in a different _____.

A. mean   B. method

C. way   D. path

67. Would you give me a hand? I really had trouble _____ the problems.

A. solving   B. to solve

C. solve   D. to solve

68. The discussion went _____ this and it went too far back to be meaningful.

A. out of   B. beyond

C. on with   D. on

69. A number of students _____ participating in the sports meeting.

A. are   B. is   C. /   D. was

70. The number of the girls _____ sharply in this school.

A. reduce   B. to reduce

C. reduces   D. are reducing

71. As we all know, hard work can contribute _____ one's success.

A. to   B. on

C. at   D. about

72. At college, students not only learn how to study _____ their own, but also learn how to get _____ with others.

A. on, /   B. /, on

C. along, on   D. on, along

73. _____ most cases, the theory is right.

A. Under   B. At   C. In   D. With

74. _____ our parents' eye, we are always the children.

A. Inside   B. At   C. On   D. In

75. Since the new law took effect, the public have reacted violently _____ this law.

A. against   B. for   C. with   D. to

76. The increasing number of private cars has a great _____ on the environment.

A. effect   B. affect

C. attitude   D. effective

77. The movie became suddenly successful because it impressed the audience strongly _____ their memories.

    A. at   B. in   C. by   D. on

78. Busy as we are, we should set _____ some time to relax ourselves.

    A. aside   B. up   C. out   D. off

79. We highly recommended that you _____ to the doctor.

    A. went   B. had gone   C. go   D. to go

80. She was good _____ Ping-Pong, and won several games.

    A. at   B. on   C. in   D. /

Part Five　Short Answer Questions

Directions: *In this part there is a short passage with five questions or incomplete statements. Read the passage carefully. Then answer the questions or complete the statement in the fewest possible words.*

Henry John Kaiser (May 9, 1882-August 24, 1967) was an American industrialist was born on May 9, 1882. He was best known as the father of modern American ship-building.

Beginning as a cashier in a dry-goods shop in Utica, New York, Kaiser moved many times as he pursued the photographic and hardware businesses, finally settling in Vancouver, British Columbia, Canada. In 1906, he moved to the West Coast. The Henry J. Kaiser Company, Ltd. was established in Vancouver, B.C., in 1914. Early successes included one of international scope, building the first concrete paved roadways in Cuba in 1915. In 1921 Kaiser won his first California paving contract and established headquarters in Oakland, California. He then profited by building the expanding public road network.

In 1923, he started Kaiser Sand and Gravel. Kaiser made the unique move of painting the trucks pink since that was his wife's favorite color.

Through an unusual management structure stressing good pay for workers, Kaiser was able to bring the road paving contract in under budget and earlier than deadline. Kaiser partnered with Bechtel Corporation to form one of the Six Companies which collectively bid on and completed the Hoover Dam on the Colorado River. The success of this massive project, which was completed two years early, led to more government road building and other infrastructure contracts such as the building of the Bonneville, Grand Coulee, and Shasta Dams, natural gas pipelines in the Southwest, Mississippi River levees, and the San Francisco-Oakland Bay Bridge underwater foundations.

After WWII, as a real estate magnate, Kaiser was the founder of the Honolulu suburban community of Hawaii Kai in Hawaii (where there is a public high school named in his honor) and Panorama City near Los Angeles.

In 1948, Kaiser established the Henry J. Kaiser Family Foundation, (also known as Kaiser Family Foundation), a U. S.-based, non-profit, private operating foundation focusing on the major health care issues facing the nation. The Foundation, not associated with Kaiser Permanente or Kaiser Industries, is an independent voice and source of facts and analysis for policymakers, the media, the health care community, and the general public. Henry Kaiser spent much of his later years in Honolulu and developed an obsession with perfecting its urban landscape.

81. What was Henry John Kaiser famous for?

82. What was Henry John Kaiser's first job?

83. Why did Henry John Kaiser paint the trunks pink?

84. What did Kaiser Family Foundation focus on?

85. What did Henry John Kaiser do in his later years?

Part Six   Translation

Directions: *Finish the sentences on Answer Sheet by translating into English.*

86. 他的债务已到几百万美元了,现在没钱偿付那些债务。(amount to)

87. 任何国家无权干涉其他国家的内政。(interfere with)

88. 汽车尾气导致全球变暖。(contribute to)

89. 他发现很难跟自己的舍友相处。(get along with)

90. 因为天气原因,飞往悉尼的航班被迫取消了。(due to)

91. 在多年努力之后,他的梦想终于变成了现实。(come true)

92. 她一回家就开始做家务。(go about)

93. 俗话说:"近朱者赤,近墨者黑。"意思是说,环境能影响,甚至塑造一个人的性格。
    (shape)

94. 这幅画应该追溯到 16 世纪。(trace)

95. 仰望天空,我们看到一头老鹰正在天空中翱翔。(soar)

Answer Sheet 1

Part One　Writing

Part Two Listening Comprehension
Section C

Sigmund Freud, an __(21)__ physician was born on May 6, __(22)__ . He __(23)__ the __(24)__ of psychology. Freud is best __(25)__ for his __(26)__ of the unconscious mind. He __(27)__ his theory through a __(28)__ form of dialogue between a __(29)__ and a psychoanalyst. He is also __(30)__ for his redefinition of sexual __(31)__ as the primary motivational __(32)__ of human life. It is __(33)__ toward a wide variety of __(34)__ , as well as his unique __(35)__ , including the use of __(36)__ association, and the interpretation of __(37)__ as sources of __(38)__ into unconscious desires. He __(39)__ away on __(40)__ 23, 1939.

Part Five Short Answer Questions

81. _____

_____

82. _____

_____

83. _____

_____

84. _____

_____

85. _____

_____

Part Six Translation

86. _____

_____

_____

87. _____

_____

88. _____

89.

90.

91.

92.

93.

94.

95.

Answer Sheet 2

Part Two   Listening Comprehension
Section A

1	2	3	4	5	6	7	8	9	10

Section B

11	12	13	14	15	16	17	18	19	20

Part Three   Reading Comprehension
Section A

41	42	43	44	45	46	47	48	49	50

Section B

51	52	53	54	55	56	57	58	59	60

Part Four   Vocabulary

61	62	63	64	65	66	67	68	69	70
71	72	73	74	75	76	77	78	79	80

Model Test 9

Part One Writing

Directions: *For this part, you are allowed 30 minutes to write a composition on the topic given in English. You should write at least 100 words.*

Say No to Terrorism

1. "9·11"恐怖袭击以来,打击恐怖活动成为各国工作的重中之重;

2. 全球各国应如何联合起来打击恐怖分子;

3. 呼吁各国敢于向恐怖活动说"不"。

Part Two Listening Comprehension

Section A

Directions: *In this section you will hear 10 short conversations. At the end of each conversation, a question will be asked about what was said, both the conversation and the question will be spoken only once. After each question there will be a pause. During the pause, you must read the four choices marked A, B, C and D, and decide which is the best answer. Then mark the corresponding letter on the Answer sheet with a single line through the center.*

1. A. 120 minutes.
   B. 135 minutes.
   C. 145 minutes.
   D. 150 minutes.

2. A. Pop music.
   B. Light music.
   C. Rock and roll.
   D. Jazz music.

3. A. She's not good at swimming.
   B. She doesn't like swimming.
   C. She likes playing soccer.
   D. She likes playing basketball.

4. A. N70.
B. N 72.

C. N 73.
D. N 95.

5. A. 5,000.
B. 2,000.

C. 30,000.
D. 20,000.

6. A. 2,000.
B. 1,500.

C. 3,500.
D. 4,000.

7. A. Apartment with one bedroom.

B. Apartment with two bedrooms.

C. Apartment with three bedrooms.

D. Villa.

8. A. Bad weather.
B. Technical problems.

C. Traffic jam.
D. The pilot.

9. A. Spicy chicken.
B. Spicy chicken.

C. Spicy pork.
D. Pork with peppers.

10. A. 15 minutes.
B. 10 minutes.

C. 5 minutes.
D. 20 minutes.

Section B

Directions: *In this section, you will hear three short passages. At the end of each passage, you will hear some questions. Both the passage and the questions will be spoken only once. After you hear a question, you must choose the best answer from the four choices marked A, B, C and D, and decide which is the best answer. Then mark the corresponding letter on the Answer Sheet with a single line through the center.*

Passage One

11. A. On April 12, 1898.

B. On April 20, 1898.

C. On April 12, 1889.

D. On April 20, 1889.

12. A. High.
B. Excellent.

C. Good.
D. Poor.

13. A. In 1905.
B. In 1906.

116

C. In 1907.   D. In 1908.

Passage Two

14. A. In 1913.   B. In 1914.
    C. In 1915.   D. In 1916.
15. A. Joining the army.
    B. Serving the war.
    C. Evading Austrian military service.
    D. Receiving better education.
16. A. In 1913.   B. In 1914.
    C. In 1915.   D. In 1916.

Passage Three

17. A. On April 26, 1945.
    B. On April 27, 1945.
    C. On April 30, 1945.
    D. On April 28, 1945.
18. A. Suicide by gunshot.
    B. Poisoning.
    C. Suicide by gunshot and poisoning.
    D. Hanging himself.
19. A. In Russia.   B. In America.
    C. In Germany.   D. In France.
20. A. Buried.   B. Unclear.
    C. Burnt.   D. Cremated.

Section C

Directions: *In this section, you will hear a passage of about 100 words three times. The passage is printed on your Answer Sheet with about 20 words missing. First you will hear the whole passage from the beginning to the end just to get a general idea of it. Then, in the second reading, you will hear a signal indicating the beginning of a pause after each sentence, sometimes two sentences or just part of a sentence. During the pause, you must write down the* *missing words you have just heard in the corresponding space on the Answer Sheet. There is also a different signal indicating the end of the pause. When you hear this signal, you must get ready for what comes next from the recording. You can check what you have written when the passage is read to you once again without the pauses.*

World War I, also known as the First World War, the Great War, and The War to End All Wars, was a ___(21)___ war which took ___(22)___ primarily in ___(23)___ from 1914 to ___(24)___ . World War I was finally over in 1918. This first global ___(25)___ had claimed from 9 ___(26)___ to 13 million lives and ___(27)___ unprecedented ___(28)___ . Germany had formally ___(29)___ on ___(30)___ 11, 1918, and all ___(31)___ had agreed to stop ___(32)___ while the terms of ___(33)___ were negotiated. On June 28, 1919, ___(34)___ and the Allied Nations, including Britain, France, Italy and ___(35)___ signed the Treaty of Versailles, formally ___(36)___ the war. Versailles is a city in France, 10 miles outside of ___(37)___ . The United States did not ___(38)___ the treaty, however, because it ___(39)___ to its terms, specifically, the high price that Germany was to pay for its role as aggressor. Instead, the U.S. ___(40)___ its own settlement with Germany in 1921.

Part Three Reading Comprehension

Section A

Directions: *In this section, there is a passage with 10 blanks. You are required to select one word for each blank from a list of choices given in a word bank following the passage. Read the passage through carefully before making your choices. Each choice in the bank is identified by a letter. Please mark the corresponding letter for each item on Answer Sheet with a single line through the center.* **You may not use any of words in the bank more than once.**

Word Bank

A. aircrafts	C. attack	E. damaged	G. destroyed	I. bombing
B. Base	D. called	F. planes	H. surprise	J. Harbor

During WWII, the Japanese attacked Pearl __(41)__ on December 7, 1941. President Franklin Roosevelt __(42)__ December 7, 1941, "a date which will live in infamy (声名狼藉)." On that day, Japanese __(43)__ attacked the United States Naval __(44)__ at Pearl Harbor, Hawaii Territory. The __(45)__ killed more than 2,300 Americans. It completely __(46)__ the American battleship U.S.S. Arizona and capsized the U.S.S. Oklahoma. The __(47)__ also sank three other ships, __(48)__ many vessels, and demolished 180 __(49)__ . The attack took the country by __(50)__ , especially the ill-prepared Pearl Harbor base.

Section B

Directions: *There are 2 passages in this section. Each passage is followed by some questions or unfinished statements. For each of them there are four choices marked A, B, C and D. You should decide on the best choice and mark the corresponding letter on Answer Sheet with a single line through the center.*

Passage One

The century from 1815 to 1914 was one of the most peaceful in European history. This was largely because European powers were preoccupied with internal political events and economic developments (industrialization) which gave them the power and scope to expand their colonial empires without getting too much in each other's way. However, the same forces that kept Europe tranquil in the 1800's also carried the seeds for trouble in the first half of the 1900's, making it a time of war, revolution, and economic turmoil.

The spread of the Industrial Revolution outside of Britain after 1850 expanded the consumer markets available for businesses to exploit. But it also expanded the number of producers competing for those markets, triggering more competition for what seemed to be a stagnant economy by the turn of the century.

European nations did two things to protect themselves. First, they (especially France, Britain, and Germany) joined in the rush for overseas colonies. The second strategy was the use of protective tariffs (import taxes) to raise the cost of foreign goods and make the home nation's goods correspondingly more appealing to its consumers.

Nationalism created other problems. The unification of Italy and especially Germany upset the balance of power in central Europe, replacing many small and vulnerable states with two unified and aggressive nations. Germany's rapid rise as a political, economic, and military giant alarmed its neighbors, particularly France, still burning to avenge its humiliating defeat in the Franco-Prussian War. Nations reacted in two ways: the formation of alliances and military build-ups.

On June 28, 1914, Gavrilo Princip, a young member of a Serbian terrorist group known as the Black Hand, murdered the heir apparent of Austria, Franz Ferdinand, and his wife in Sarajevo, Austria. Naturally, this created quite a stir in the papers, but few at that time saw it as important enough to lead to a general war. However, behind the scenes, all the forces of nationalist rivalries, economic competition, military buildups, and interlocking alliances were blowing this murder way out of proportion and driving events wildly out of control and toward war. Finally the war broke out.

Questions 51 to 55 are based on the passage.

51. From 1815 to 1914, what kind of period was Europe in?

   A. Most peaceful.

   B. Most disturbing.

   C. A period of turmoil.

   D. Fast developing.

52. Which of the following is NOT what the European powers did during a century before WWI?

   A. Focus on internal political events.

   B. Develop economy.

   C. Fight against each other.

   D. Expand their colonial empires.

53. What caused the expansion of the consumer markets in Europe?

   A. The Industrial Revolution.

   B. The expansion of colonies.

   C. Development of national powers.

   D. Economic Development.

54. Which of the following does NOT belong to the measures the European nations took to protect themselves?

   A. Struggle for more colonies.

120

B. Fight for more markets.

C. Use the protective import taxes.

D. Make their products competitive.

55. What caused the imbalance of power in Europe?

A. Economic development.

B. The Industrial Revolution.

C. The unification of Germany.

D. Murder of heir apparent of Austria and his wife.

Passage Two

Benito Mussolini's rise to power was rapid; his Fascist Party Blackshirts marched into Rome in 1922, a year before Hitler's failed first attempt to seize power, the Munich Beer Hall Putch, landed the German in prison. By the time Hitler became the leader of Germany, Mussolini had been leader of Italy for more than ten years. His ambition was to regain for Italy the prestige and power.

Benito Mussolini served in the First World War as a young man and dreamed of military glory in a Second War to come. Both returned from the First World War to find their countries in political and economic chaos and formed extremist political parties.

His biggest mistake, however, was the decision to enter the Second World War. On 10 June 1940, Germany had been at war with Britain and France since the previous September, but Italy was still at peace, and had little reason to fear that any of the other powers would attack it. Germany was on the verge of winning the Battle of France, and France was likely to surrender very soon, and it seemed to many observers that Britain would then make peace. Perhaps Mussolini thought that Italy would be the next target for Nazi aggression, if he did not help Hitler win; or he may have just been moved to grab a piece of France before it was too late. In any case, he did declare war on France.

By July 1943, Italy had lost all of it colonies in Africa, and most of its army, and was being invaded. Mussolini was relieved of his leadership by a revolt within his own Fascist Grand Council, and Victor Emmanuael III, the King of Italy, who had been reduced to a figurehead by Mussolini, appointed Marshal Badoglio to be the new Prime Minister. Mussolini was arrested, while Italy attempted to change sides. In the southern part of Italy, occupied by the Allies, this succeeded, and the new Italian government helped create the Italian Co-Belligerent Forces.

Hitler sent German paratroops to rescue Mussolini from the mountaintop resort where he was imprisoned. He then set up the Italian Social Republic in German-held northern Italy, with Mussolini as its leader.

When the Germans surrendered in northern Italy, in April, 1945, Mussolini was arrested again. He and his mistress, Clara Petacci, were removed from the jail at Giulino di Messegra and lynched, by the local Communist partisans.

Questions 56 to 60 are based on the passage.

56. How long did Benito Mussolini come into power before Hitler became leader of Germany?

    A. More than ten years.　　　　　B. One year.

    C. Two years.　　　　　　　　　D. Seven years.

57. What was the biggest mistake Mussolini made?

    A. Supporting Hitler.

    B. Being the leader of Italy.

    C. Being defeated in WWII.

    D. Decision to enter the Second World War.

58. When did Italy lose all his territories in Africa?

    A. By July 1942.　　　　　　　B. By July 1945.

    C. By July 1944.　　　　　　　D. By July 1943.

59. How many times was Mussolini arrested in his life?

    A. 1.　　　　　B. 2.　　　　　C. 3.　　　　　D. 4.

60. What did the text mainly talk about?

    A. Mussolini and Hitler.

    B. Mussolini and the WWII.

    C. Mussolini and his life.

    D. Mussolini and his wife.

Part Four　Vocabulary

Directions: *For this part you are required to choose the best answer from A, B, C and D to complete the following sentences.*

61. He gave me a _____ description of what happened that day.

    A. detailed　　　　　　　　　B. detailing

C. detail   D. in detail

62. Finally they realized that the victory was close at _____ and they needed to prepare for it.

    A. corner   B. foot

    C. hand   D. arm

63. It seems to rain. They tried to _____ shelter as soon as possible.

    A. seek   B. find

    C. look for   D. find out

64. He lived in the isolated island for many years, separating himself _____ the outside world.

    A. of   B. on

    C. from   D. out of

65. They wonder why she had her pet dog _____.

    A. poison   B. poisoning

    C. to poison   D. poisoned

66. After they were rescued, they felt _____ sense of relief.

    A. titanic   B. big

    C. large   D. enormous

67. The sight at the pests robbed her of the appetite _____ food.

    A. at   B. for

    C. after   D. in

68. They achieved their goals because they succeeded in _____ their plans.

    A. carrying out   B. carry out

    C. carry on   D. to carry on

69. With you _____ charge, I feel at ease.

    A. on   B. by

    C. in   D. with

70. He said he still had some difficulties _____ the business.

    A. running   B. to run

    C. have run   D. to run

71. In the _____, he finished all housework and went out for a walk.

    A. meanwhile   B. meantime

    C. mean   D. time

72. He thought his parents should have _____ a spectacle of themselves in public.

    A. gone   B. got

    C. made   D. taken

73. The criminal was brought to justice and finally met his _____.

    A. aim   B. death

    C. goal   D. end

74. The final exam is coming soon. Let's _____ well preparation for it.

    A. make   B. take

    C. get   D. carry

75. The man was praised for being loyal _____ his country.

    A. of   B. on

    C. to   D. in

76. _____ word came that our team won the game at last.

    A. /   B. The

    C. A   D. Their

77. He had to retire _____ the air-raid shelter after being defeated.

    A. on   B. in

    C. to   D. into

78. The news that he regained his consciousness was a great relief _____ his family.

    A. on   B. at

    C. in   D. to

79. Although he was strict _____ his students, Mr. Wang won students' respect.

    A. with   B. at

    C. on   D. from

80. The matter is closely associated _____ what he said.

    A. at   B. on

    C. with   D. in

Part Five   Short Answer Questions

Directions: *In this part there is a short passage with five questions or incomplete statements. Read the passage carefully. Then answer the questions or complete the statement in the fewest possible words.*

As I did not consider that I could take responsibility, during the years of struggle, of contracting a marriage, I have now decided, before the closing of my earthly career, to take as my wife that girl who, after many years of faithful friendship, entered, of her own free will, the practically besieged town in order to share her destiny with me. At her own desire she goes as my wife with me into death. It will compensate us for what we both lost through my work in the service of my people.

What I possess belongs — in so far as it has any value — to the Party. Should this no longer exist, to the State; should the State also be destroyed, no further decision of mine is necessary.

My paintings, in the collections which I have bought in the course of years, have never been collected for private purposes, but only for the extension of a gallery in my home town of Linz on Donau.

It is my most sincere wish that this bequest may be duly executed.

I nominate as my Executor my most faithful Party comrade, Martin Bormann.

He is given full legal authority to make all decisions.

He is permitted to take out everything that has a sentimental value or is necessary for the maintenance of a modest simple life, for my brothers and sisters, also above all for the mother of my wife and my faithful co-workers who are well known to him, principally my old Secretaries Frau Winter etc. who have for many years aided me by their work.

I myself and my wife — in order to escape the disgrace of deposition or capitulation — choose death. It is our wish to be burnt immediately on the spot where I have carried out the greatest part of my daily work in the course of a twelve years' service to my people.

Given in Berlin, 29th April 1945, 4:00 A.M.

[Signed] A. Hitler

[Witnesses]

Dr. Joseph Goebbels

Martin Bormann

Colonel Nicholaus von Below

81. What's the probable title of the passage?

82. Who had the right to make all decisions on Hitler's property after his death?

83. Where would the paintings Hitler collected be sent?

84. How long was Adolf Hitler in power in Germany?

85. What would Hitler and his wife probably do after finishing this document?

Part Six Translation

Directions: *Finish the sentences on Answer Sheet by translating into English.*

86. 这个人做了很多坏事,突然在一天晚上死在自己家里。(meet one's end)

87. 他被起诉犯有谋杀罪,将会在公共场合吊死。(string up)

88. 当我正在大街上走的时候,杰克挥舞着他的手,示意我到他的店里去。(call in)

89. 当他们回家后,发现小偷闯进了他们的家。(break in)

90. 由于压力越来越大,他病倒了。(build up)

91. 在这期间,他已经学会了几种外语。(meantime)

92. 总经理不在的时候,副总经理将主持工作。(in charge of)

93. 当我有空的时候,我总是叫几个朋友过来打牌。(round up)

94. 我希望我们尽快完成这份工作。(have done with)

95. 我们已经整四年没有见面了。(to the day)

Answer Sheet 1

Part One   Writing

_____
_____
_____
_____
_____
_____
_____
_____
_____
_____
_____
_____
_____
_____
_____
_____
_____
_____
_____
_____
_____
_____
_____
_____
_____
_____

Part Two   Listening Comprehension

Section C

World War I, also known as the First World War, the Great War, and The War to End All Wars, was a ___(21)___ war which took ___(22)___ primarily in ___(23)___ from 1914 to ___(24)___ . World War I was finally over in 1918. This first global ___(25)___ had claimed from 9 ___(26)___ to 13 million lives and ___(27)___ unprecedented ___(28)___ . Germany had formally ___(29)___ on ___(30)___ 11, 1918, and all ___(31)___ had agreed to stop ___(32)___ while the terms of ___(33)___ were negotiated. On June 28, 1919, ___(34)___ and the Allied Nations, including Britain, France, Italy and ___(35)___ signed the Treaty of Versailles, formally ___(36)___ the war. Versailles is a city in France, 10 miles outside of ___(37)___ . The United States did not ___(38)___ the treaty, however, because it ___(39)___ to its terms, specifically, the high price that Germany was to pay for its role as aggressor. Instead, the U.S. ___(40)___ its own settlement with Germany in 1921.

Part Five   Short Answer Questions

81. _____

_____

82. _____

_____

83. _____

_____

84. _____

_____

85. _____

_____

Part Six   Translation

86. _____

_____

_____

87. _____
_____
_____

88. _____
_____
_____

89. _____
_____
_____

90. _____
_____
_____

91. _____
_____
_____

92. _____
_____
_____

93. _____
_____
_____

94. _____
_____
_____

95. _____
_____
_____

Answer Sheet 2

Part Two Listening Comprehension

Section A

1	2	3	4	5	6	7	8	9	10

Section B

11	12	13	14	15	16	17	18	19	20

Part Three Reading Comprehension

Section A

41	42	43	44	45	46	47	48	49	50

Section B

51	52	53	54	55	56	57	58	59	60

Part Four Vocabulary

61	62	63	64	65	66	67	68	69	70

71	72	73	74	75	76	77	78	79	80

Model Test 10

Part One   Writing

Directions: *For this part, you are allowed 30 minutes to write a composition on the topic given in English. You should write at least 100 words.*

The Benefits of Scientific Development

1. 现在,科技的发展日新月异,改变着人们生活和工作的方方面面;
2. 科技发展的原因;
3. 这种发展对于社会和人们带来的好处。

Part Two   Listening Comprehension

Section A

Directions: *In this section you will hear 10 short conversations. At the end of each conversation, a question will be asked about what was said, both the conversation and the question will be spoken only once. After each question there will be a pause. During the pause, you must read the four choices marked A, B, C and D, and decide which is the best answer. Then mark the corresponding letter on the Answer sheet with a single line through the center.*

1. A. 100 Yuan.   B. 200 Yuan.
   C. 400 Yuan.   D. 500 Yuan.
2. A. To the classroom.   B. To the library.
   C. To the gym.   D. To the playground.
3. A. Small.   B. Smaller.
   C. Larger.   D. Large.
4. A. 120.   B. 80.   C. 160.   D. 40.
5. A. 98.   B. 100.   C. 101.   D. 99.

6. A. The 1st prize.　　　　　　　B. The 4th prize.

　　C. The 3rd prize.　　　　　　　D. The 2nd prize.

7. A. This afternoon.　　　　　　　B. Tomorrow.

　　C. Wednesday morning.　　　　　D. Wednesday afternoon.

8. A. A room with double bed on July 4th.

　　B. A room with double bed on July 3rd.

　　C. A room with single bed on July 4th.

　　D. A room with single bed on July 3rd.

9. A. 6.　　　　　B. 10.　　　　　C. 5.　　　　　D. 1.

10. A. 1.　　　　　B. 2.　　　　　C. 3.　　　　　D. 4.

Section B

Directions: *In this section, you will hear three short passages. At the end of each passage, you will hear some questions. Both the passage and the questions will be spoken only once. After you hear a question, you must choose the best answer from the four choices marked A, B, C and D, and decide which is the best answer. Then mark the corresponding letter on the Answer Sheet with a single line through the center.*

Passage One

11. A. In France.　　　　　　　　　B. In England.

　　C. In Italy.　　　　　　　　　　D. In Germany.

12. A. In the late 18th century.

　　B. In the early 18th century.

　　C. In the early 19th century.

　　D. In the middle of the 19th century.

13. A. Steam Engine.　　　　　　　B. Electrical power.

　　C. Car.　　　　　　　　　　　　D. Railway.

Passage Two

14. A. His poor health.　　　　　　B. His poor family.

　　C. His cruel father.　　　　　　D. His mother.

15. A. Pump.　　　　　　　　　　　B. Railway.

C. Light bulb.   D. Steam engine.

16. A. Electrical power.   B. Electronics.

      C. Engineering.   D. Metrical.

Passage Three

17. A. In 1896.   B. In 1886.

      C. In 1867.   D. In 1876.

18. A. Antonio Meucci.   B. Havana.

      C. Watson.   D. Bell.

19. A. In 1871.   B. In 1876.

      C. In 1848.   D. In 1875.

20. A. Poor health.

      B. Lack of money.

      C. Not knowing that.

      D. There was no patent at that time.

Section C

Directions: *In this section, you will hear a passage of about 100 words three times. The passage is printed on your Answer Sheet with about 20 words missing. First you will hear the whole passage from the beginning to the end just to get a general idea of it. Then, in the second reading, you will hear a signal indicating the beginning of a pause after each sentence, sometimes two sentences or just part of a sentence. During the pause, you must write down the missing words you have just heard in the corresponding space on the Answer Sheet. There is also a different signal indicating the end of the pause. When you hear this signal, you must get ready for what comes next from the recording. You can check what you have written when the passage is read to you once again without the pauses.*

Sir Charles Spencer Chaplin, was born on 16 April, ___(21)___, better known as Charlie Chaplin, was an Academy Award-winning English comedic ___(22)___. Chaplin became one of the most ___(23)___ actors as well as a notable ___(24)___, composer and ___(25)___ in the early to mid ___(26)___ cinema era. He is ___(27)___ to have been one of the __(28)__ mimes and clowns ever caught on film and has greatly __(29)__ performers in this field. His working life in __(30)__ spanned over __(31)__ years, from the Victorian __(32)__ and music hall in the United Kingdom as a child __(33)__ almost until his death at the age of __(34)__ . Chaplin is also one of the co-founders of United Artists, the movie __(35)__ that revolutionized Hollywood.

Chaplin's principal __(36)__ was "The Tramp". "The Tramp" is a vagrant with the refined __(37)__ and dignity of a __(38)__ . The character wears a __(39)__ coat, oversized trousers and shoes, and a derby; carries a __(40)__ cane; and has a signature toothbrush moustache.

Part Three   Reading Comprehension

Section A

Directions: *In this section, there is a passage with 10 blanks. You are required to select one word for each blank from a list of choices given in a word bank following the passage. Read the passage through carefully before making your choices. Each choice in the bank is identified by a letter. Please mark the corresponding letter for each item on Answer Sheet with a single line through the center.* **You may not use any of words in the bank more than once.**

Word Bank

A. father	C. global	E. founder	G. administration	I. inventor
B. commitment	D. production	F. revolutionized	H. technical	J. richest

Henry Ford, born on July 30, 1863, was the American __(41)__ of the Ford Motor Company and __(42)__ of modern assembly lines used in mass __(43)__ . His introduction of the Model T automobile __(44)__ transportation and American industry. He was a prolific __(45)__ and was awarded 161 U.S. patents. As owner of the Ford Company he became one of the __(46)__ and best-known people in the world. Ford had a __(47)__ vision, with consumerism as the key to peace. Ford did not believe in accountants; he amassed one of the world's largest fortunes without ever having his company audited under his __(48)__ . Henry Ford's intense __(49)__ to lowering costs resulted in many __(50)__ and business innovations.

Section B

Directions: *There are 2 passages in this section. Each passage is followed by some questions or unfinished statements. For each of them there are four choices marked A, B, C and D. You should decide on the best choice and mark the corresponding letter on Answer Sheet with a single line through the center.*

Passage One

The Second Industrial Revolution is a phrase used by some historians to describe an assumed second phase of the Industrial Revolution. Since this period includes the rise of industrial powers other than France and Britain, such as Germany or the USA, it may be used by writers who want to stress the contribution of these countries or relativize the position of the UK.

The second industrial revolution is termed the second phase of the Industrial Revolution, since from a technological and a social point of view there is no clean break between the first Industrial Revolution and the Second Industrial Revolution. Indeed, it might be argued that it branches from the middle of the nineteenth century with the growth of railways and steam ships, for crucial inventions such as the Bessemer and Siemens open hearth furnace steel making processes were invented in the decades *preceding* 1871, producing cheaper steel which allowed cheaper, quicker steam transport.

In the United States of America the Second Industrial Revolution is commonly associated with electrification as pioneered by Nikola Tesla, Thomas Alva Edison and George Westinghouse and by scientific management as applied by Frederick Winslow Taylor.

In the past, the term "second industrial revolution" has also often been used in the popular press and by technologists or industrialists to refer to the changes following the spread of new technology after World War I. The excitement and the debate over the dangers and the benefits of the Atomic Age were more intense and lasting than those over the Space age but they both were perceived (separately or together) to lead to another industrial revolution. At the start of the 21st century the term "second industrial revolution" has also been used to describe the anticipated effects of hypothetical molecular nanotechnology systems upon society. In this more recent scenario, the nanofactory would render the majority of today's modern manufacturing processes obsolete, vastly impacting all facets of the modern economy. This article refers exclusively to the earlier period.

Industrial revolutions may also be renumbered by taking earlier developments, such as the rise of medieval technology in the 12th century, or of ancient Chinese technology during the Tang Dynasty, or of ancient Roman technology, as first.

Questions 51 to 55 are based on the passage.

51. Which country became powerful during the Second Industrial Revolution?

    A. France.　　　　　　　　　B. Germany.

    C. Italy.　　　　　　　　　　D. England.

52. When did the Second Industrial Revolution roughly begin?

    A. In the early nineteenth century.

    B. In the late nineteenth century.

    C. In the middle of the nineteenth century.

    D. In the first half of the nineteenth century.

53. What does the word "*preceding*" mean in the second Paragraph?

    A. Before.　　　　　　　　　B. After.

    C. In.　　　　　　　　　　　D. During.

54. What benefited U.S.A. during the Second Industrial Revolution?

    A. Engineering.　　　　　　　B. Use of Steam Engine.

    C. Electrification.　　　　　　D. Mechanism.

55. What does the passage mainly talk about?

    A. Brief introduction of the Second Industrial Revolution.

    B. Inventions in the Second Industrial Revolution.

    C. U.S development during the Second Industrial Revolution.

    D. Development of Germany during the Second Industrial Revolution.

Passage Two

When Spanish explorers first entered the area now known as Hollywood, Native Americans were living in the canyons of the Santa Monica Mountains. Before long, the Indians had been moved to missions and the land which Hollywood now occupies was divided in two by the Spanish Government. Acreage to the west became part of Rancho La Brea (牧场) and settlements to the East became Rancho Los Feliz.

By the 1870s an agricultural community flourished in the area and crops ranging from hay and grain to subtropical(亚热带) bananas and pineapples were thriving. During the 1880s, the Ranchos were sub-divided. In 1886, H. H. Wilcox bought an area of Rancho La Brea that his wife then christened "Hollywood." Within a few years, Wilcox had devised a grid plan for his new community, paved Prospect Avenue (now Hollywood Boulevard) for his main street and was selling large residential lots to wealthy Midwest-erners looking to build homes so they could "winter in California."

Prospect Avenue soon became a prestigious residential street populated with large Queen Anne, Victorian, and Mission Revival houses. Mrs. Daeida Wilcox raised funds to build churches, schools and a library and Hollywood quickly became a complete and prosperous community. The community incorporated in 1903, but its independence was short-lived, as the lack of water forced annexation in 1910 to the city of Los Angeles, which had a surplus supply of water.

In 1911, the Nestor Company opened Hollywood's first film studio in an old tavern on the corner of Sunset and Gower. Not long thereafter Cecil B. DeMille and D. W. Griffith began making movies in the area drawn to the community for its open space and moderate climate.

Questions 56 to 60 are based on the passage.

56. Who first explored the today's Hollywood?

    A. Dutch.   B. Portuguese.

    C. Italian.   D. Spanish.

57. When did Hollywood get its present name?

    A. In 1910.   B. In 1886.

    C. In 1911.   D. In 1903.

58. When did Hollywood become a complete and prosperous community?

    A. In 1886.   B. In 1910.

    C. In 1911.   D. In 1903.

59. Why was Hollywood forced to be annexed to the city Los Angeles?

    A. Lack of water.

    B. Lack of fund.

    C. Small number of population.

    D. Natural Disaster.

60. When was Hollywood's first film studio established?

    A. In 1886.   B. In 1910.

C. In 1911.   D. In 1903.

Part Four   Vocabulary

Directions: *For this part you are required to choose the best answer from A, B, C and D to complete the following sentences.*

61. Hurry up! Let's _____ our pace, otherwise we'll be late for class.

     A. quick   B. quicken

     C. quickening   D. quickly

62. An idea suddenly occurred _____ me that we would go outing this weekend.

     A. on   B. at   C. to   D. toward

63. Smoke is harmful to your health because it may lead _____ lung cancer.

     A. to   B. on   C. with   D. as

64. The driver was fined $ 50 for _____ the speed limit.

     A. exceeding   B. exceed

     C. surpassing   D. surpass

65. It is necessary that the companies should catch up _____ the changing technology.

     A. behind   B. /   C. with   D. on

66. As times went _____, the man realized that his friend would never come back.

     A. far   B. out   C. on   D. by

67. Now, Internet is available _____ almost everyone in the cities.

     A. at   B. to   C. by   D. with

68. _____ the help of the dictionary, I succeeded in understanding this sentence.

     A. As   B. On   C. With   D. Under

69. It _____ two years for experts to put this theory into practice.

     A. takes   B. gets   C. makes   D. spends

70. There is a _____ difference between the recorder and digital video.

     A. strike   B. stricken

     C. striking   D. sticking

71. The rocket flied into the sky at an _____ speed.

     A. to astonish   B. astonished

     C. astonishing   D. astonish

72. Pigeon is the _____ of peace.

A. symbol   B. sign

C. signal   D. symbolic

73. With the technology _____, people live a more comfortable life.

A. advances   B. advancing

C. advanced   D. is advancing

74. He applied _____ studying abroad, but in vain at last.

A. for   B. on   C. at   D. about

75. The villa he is living in is in beautiful _____.

A. environments   B. circumstances

C. surroundings   D. surrounding

76. It is essential that people in this area _____ immediately.

A. evacuated

B. were evacuated

C. evacuate

D. be evacuated

77. Lack of money should be taken into _____ when we discuss the project.

A. account   B. accounting

C. accountant   D. regard

78. It took her a _____ 20 minutes to finish her homework.

A. merely   B. mere

C. only   D. at least

79. He arrived at the top of the mountain and had _____ sickness.

A. height   B. attitude

C. altitude   D. fortitude

80. This machine is used to _____ the power.

A. result   B. manufacture

C. cause   D. generate

Part Five   Short Answer Questions

Directions: *In this part there is a short passage with five questions or incomplete statements. Read the passage carefully. Then answer the questions or complete the statement in the fewest possible words.*

The event which many historians of science call the scientific revolution can be dated roughly as having begun in 1543, the year in which Nicolaus Copernicus published his *On the Revolutions of the Heavenly Spheres* and Andreas Vesalius published his *On the Fabric of the Human body*. As with many historical demarcations, historians of science disagree about its boundaries. Although the period is commonly dated to the 16th and 17th centuries, some see elements contributing to the revolution as early as the middle ages, and finding its last stages in chemistry and biology in the 18th and 19th centuries. There is general agreement, however, that the intervening period saw a fundamental transformation in scientific ideas in physics, astronomy, and biology, in institutions supporting scientific investigation, and in the more widely held picture of the universe. As a result, the scientific revolution is commonly viewed as a foundation and origin of modern science. The "Continuity Thesis" is the opposing view that there was no radical discontinuity between the development of science in the Middle Ages and later developments in the Renaissance and early modern period.

81. When did the scientific revolution roughly begin according to the passage?

82. In 1543, two important books were published, what were they?

83. What was the scientific revolution commonly viewed as by the historians?

84. Sum up the general agreement on the period of the scientific revolution.

85. What dose the passage mainly talk about?

Part Six Translation

Directions: *Finish the sentences on Answer Sheet by translating into English.*

86. 他昨天告诉我的故事使我想起了我在农村度过的童年时光。(conjure up)

87. 他们在雨中艰难前行了几个小时。(labor along)

88. 随着时间的推移,事情会变得好起来。(go by)

89. 牛以草为生。(feed on)

90. 在第一堂课上,学生们依次报出自己的姓名。(call out)

91. 现在,在发达国家,将新思想应用于实践的时间越来越短。(put to work)

92. 他们攒了10年的钱也不够他们全球旅行用的。(inadequate)

93. 这部电影因误导观众而受到谴责。(mislead)

94. 在夏天的时候,出门之前要记得涂上防晒霜。(apply)

95. 据估计,他们每年的平均收入是10万美元。(average)

Answer Sheet 1

Part One   Writing

_____
_____
_____
_____
_____
_____
_____
_____
_____
_____
_____
_____
_____
_____
_____
_____
_____
_____
_____
_____
_____
_____
_____
_____
_____

Part Two   Listening Comprehension

Section C

Sir Charles Spencer Chaplin, was born on 16 April,   (21)   , better known as Charlie Chaplin, was an Academy Award-winning English comedic   (22)   . Chaplin became one of the most   (23)   actors as well as a notable   (24)   , composer and   (25)   in the early to mid   (26)   cinema era. He is   (27)   to have been one of the   (28)   mimes and clowns ever caught on film and has greatly   (29)   performers in this field. His working life in   (30)   spanned over   (31)   years, from the Victorian   (32)   and music hall in the United Kingdom as a child   (33)   almost until his death at the age of   (34)   . Chaplin is also one of the co-founders of United Artists, the movie   (35)   that revolutionized Hollywood.

Chaplin's principal   (36)   was "The Tramp". "The Tramp" is a vagrant with the refined   (37)   and dignity of a   (38)   . The character wears a   (39)   coat, oversized trousers and shoes, and a derby; carries a   (40)   cane; and has a signature toothbrush moustache.

Part Five   Short Answer Questions

81. _____

_____

82. _____

_____

83. _____

_____

84. _____

_____

85. _____

_____

Part Six   Translation

86. _____

_____

87.

88.

89.

90.

91.

92.

93.

94.

95.

Answer Sheet 2

Part Two Listening Comprehension
Section A

1	2	3	4	5	6	7	8	9	10

Section B

11	12	13	14	15	16	17	18	19	20

Part Three Reading Comprehension
Section A

41	42	43	44	45	46	47	48	49	50

Section B

51	52	53	54	55	56	57	58	59	60

Part Four Vocabulary

61	62	63	64	65	66	67	68	69	70
71	72	73	74	75	76	77	78	79	80

Key to Model Tests

Model Test 1

Part One Writing

Car Explosion in Beijing

According to the statistics released from the Beijing Municipal Communications Commission, the number of private cars is soaring by more than 1,000 each day in Beijing, and the amount of private automobiles has surpassed 3 million in the capital recently. The car explosion, especially the explosion of the private cars has become a headache for Beijingers and city planner. This issue has generated hot debate, so opinions on it vary.

Some people highly recommend the Beijing Municipal government should take any possible measures to limit the increasing number of the private cars. They say that in recent years, traffic jams on major Beijing roads have been getting more and more frequent. At rush hour Beijing roads are one big parking lot, and that riding a bike or even walking is often faster than driving. Indeed, cars cannot move once they get stuck on the road. If no action is taken to deal with this problem, the current road network in the city will be unable to meet the ever-increasing demand for traffic facilities and the traffic condition in Beijing will be worse and worse.

However, other people are optimistic about the capital traffic issue. They believe that the authorities concerned are devoting more efforts to improving the city's traffic conditions and have achieved some results. For examples, some intersections and roads where the traffic jams often happen have become much smoother by means of being widened. As long as these measures are taken, the traffic jams in Beijing will be solved or at least be partially relieved.

In my opinion, I do believe Beijing Municipal government will successfully deal with the traffic problems and meet the traffic needs of the 29th Olympic Games by the year of

2008.

Part Two Listening Comprehension

Section A

1	2	3	4	5	6	7	8	9	10
C	A	B	C	D	A	D	B	C	A

Section B

11	12	13	14	15	16	17	18	19	20
B	D	A	C	B	D	B	A	C	A

Section C

21. divided   22. 450   23. grammar   24. from   25. Modern

26. period   27. known   28. changes   29. effect   30. vocabulary

31. Old   32. lost   33. thousands   34. borrowed   35. 1500

36. 1700   37. nineteenth   38. twentieth   39. rapid   40. history

Part Three Reading Comprehension

Section A

41	42	43	44	45	46	47	48	49	50
C	D	A	J	H	B	E	I	G	F

Section B

51	52	53	54	55	56	57	58	59	60
B	C	A	D	B	A	C	C	D	A

Part Four Vocabulary

61	62	63	64	65	66	67	68	69	70
A	B	D	B	A	C	A	D	C	A

71	72	73	74	75	76	77	78	79	80
B	C	D	A	B	B	C	A	B	A

Part Five   Short Answer Questions

81. 1863

82. Red Cross, Red Crescent

83. Humanity, impartiality, neutrality, independence, voluntary service, unity and universality.

84. To help the wounded, sick, and homeless in wartime and in the disaster. Provide help to those in need from all over the world.

85. They are comparatively independent and exercise no power over the other.

Part Six   Translation

86. What makes it rather disturbing was the <u>arbitrary</u> circumstances both of my arrest and my subsequent fate in court.

87. Nowadays, the <u>process</u> of obtaining the driver's license becomes more and more complex.

88. I have to earn much more money these days because the rent is <u>due</u> next month.

89. College students find it difficult to seek <u>employment</u> after graduation.

90. People always play a joke on his heavy southern <u>accent</u>.

91. The <u>witness</u> told the judge what had happened to the victim on that day.

92. All he did yesterday <u>confirmed</u> my belief that he was a reliable man.

93. The topic <u>revolved</u> around how to combat the terrorist attack at the meeting yesterday.

94. Everyone doesn't like Mary because she is always <u>complaining</u> about something.

95. He was punished for <u>committing</u> an error.

Model Test 2

Part One   Writing

The Best Way to Keep Fit

Nowadays, more and more people are becoming concerned about their health, or how to keep healthy. Because people are aware of the importance of good health, without which you can not do anything you want. Most of people busy themselves with a lot of work. The work load is really beyond them. They have to sit in front of the computer for

147

many hours at a stretch. After work, their head and eyes often ache, which is really harmful to their health. In my opinion, the best way to keep fit is jogging.

After a long-time study or work, you'd better have a jogging. It will help you relax yourself both physically and mentally. You can also breathe fresh air when jogging that is good to your heart. So you can keep away from the heart disease. Regular jogging enables you to have a strong body so as to work energetically.

So bear in mind that jogging is the best way to keep healthy.

Part Two   Listening Comprehension

Section A

1	2	3	4	5	6	7	8	9	10
B	C	D	A	B	A	D	B	C	A

Section B

11	12	13	14	15	16	17	18	19	20
A	C	D	B	B	D	B	B	A	C

Section C

21. New York   22. coast   23. United States   24. mouth   25. population

26. 8 million   27. largest   28. covers   29. 321   30. includes

31. 5   32. mainly   33. urban   34. area   35. business

36. entertainment   37. fashion   38. world   39. UN   40. lowest

Part Three   Reading Comprehension

Section A

41	42	43	44	45	46	47	48	49	50
E	B	A	J	F	C	I	H	G	D

Section B

51	52	53	54	55	56	57	58	59	60
B	B	A	C	D	C	D	A	C	D

Part Four   Vocabulary

61	62	63	64	65	66	67	68	69	70
A	C	D	B	A	B	D	A	C	D
71	72	73	74	75	76	77	78	79	80
C	D	A	B	C	B	C	D	A	A

Part Five Short Answer Questions

81. Because it is a nation originally made of immigrants, and the population in America is most racially and culturally diverse in the world.

82. The policy and practice of imposing the social separation of races, as in schools, housing, and industry, especially so as to practice discrimination against people of color in a predominantly white society.

83. 35.

84. In 1964. He was killed by the assassins.

85. To express you ideas about the racial problems.

Part Six Translation

86. After heard the new, he suddenly <u>flared</u> up.

87. Her job is to <u>write</u> out the content of the meeting after it finishes.

88. They <u>brushed aside</u> a number of out - dated concepts.

89. It was first-aid treatment that <u>brought</u> Jack <u>through</u>.

90. There were some of my good friends who <u>stood by</u> me, and still do.

91. The beasts at bay will <u>fight back</u>.

92. He entered the room, and <u>stumbled</u> into my arms.

93. Mary finally <u>found out</u> what really happened on that night.

94. You'd better go to a doctor as soon as possible, otherwise, your wound will be <u>infected</u>.

95. He was <u>captured</u> by the enemy and spent the rest of his life in prison.

Model Test 3

Part One Writing

My Favorite Teacher

My favorite teacher is my English teacher Ms. Zhang. She was 25 years old at that time when she taught me English in the high school. She is the best English teacher I have ever met.

Tall and pretty, she became an English teacher immediately after she graduated from the Normal University. She said she liked teaching, so she decided to be a teacher though she could find much more well-paid or comfortable job after her graduation. Both as a teacher and a friend, Ms. Zhang has always been willing and ready to answer any question we have ever asked her. And she tried to make her lesson as interesting as she could and stimulate every student and arouse our interest in English. And on the personal side, she did not hesitate to invite her students to become an extended part of her family. I appreciate this immensely.

Up to now, I still benefit a lot from her teaching. I hope I will become a teacher like her in the future.

Part Two　Listening Comprehension

Section A

1	2	3	4	5	6	7	8	9	10
A	C	D	B	C	D	B	C	B	A

Section B

11	12	13	14	15	16	17	18	19	20
B	C	A	B	D	D	B	A	B	C

Section C

21. education　　22. different　　23. system　　24. America　　25. public

26. kindergarten 27. spend　　28. attending　29. choose　　30. nursery

31. centers　　32. pre-school 33. 6　　　　34. enter　　35. 12

36. complete　　37. elementary 38. high school 39. graduate　　40. college

Part Three　Reading Comprehension

Section A

41	42	43	44	45	46	47	48	49	50
F	G	E	C	A	D	B	I	H	J

Section B

51	52	53	54	55	56	57	58	59	60
C	C	A	B	D	A	D	B	C	D

Part Four Vocabulary

61	62	63	64	65	66	67	68	69	70
D	B	A	C	D	D	A	D	A	B

71	72	73	74	75	76	77	78	79	80
B	A	C	D	A	B	B	C	D	A

Part Five Short Answer Questions

81. An occupational disease is a health problem caused by exposure to a workplace health hazard.

82. 3. First, Immediate or acute reactions, like shortness of breath or nausea, can be caused by a one-time event. Second. Gradual reactions, like asthma or dermatitis. These reactions tend to last for a longer time. Third, delayed reactions or diseases that take a long time to develop, like lung cancer or loss of hearing, can be noticed long after the job is over.

83. Occupational voice disorders.

84. Chalk dust or marker fumes.

85. Open.

Part Six Translation

86. Today he felt very tired because he <u>stayed up</u> watching the World Cup last night.

87. The point is that the students have no idea how to <u>take notes</u> in class.

88. His present success is <u>built on</u> his constant efforts.

89. A student should form a habit of <u>keeping a diary</u>.

90. We can't take this factor into consideration, <u>leaving out</u> the rest of other important factors.

91. Could you help me <u>send</u> this parcel <u>off</u> to my friend tomorrow?

92. I'm afraid they will not attend our wedding ceremony because they are busy <u>working at</u> a new invention.

93. Everyone at the meeting <u>caught their breath</u> for the announcement of the result.

94. I was <u>convinced</u> that Chinese team would win the following games.

95. It requires us to <u>reflect</u> on the contributions he made to his hometown.

Model Test 4

Part One Writing

My Attitudes toward Beggars

Today, beggars lying on the ground can be found in many parts of big cities. Some people show indifference to those poor and homeless people, while others show their sympathy to the beggars. In my opinion, I agree with the latter.

The beggars usually consist of the homeless, the disable, and elderly women. They come to the city from the poor countryside, without acquiring any practical skills. So they can't find a job, have no place to live in. In the end, they have no choice but to lie on the ground begging for food. People should be sympathetic to them. Some people may counter by saying that some of the beggars are fake ones. But most of them really need our help. The government has taken some action to help those helpless people and will continue doing so.

So don't hesitate to give out some changes to the beggars or offer some help when you come across the beggars later.

Part Two Listening Comprehension

Section A

1	2	3	4	5	6	7	8	9	10
B	C	A	C	D	D	B	A	D	A

Section B

11	12	13	14	15	16	17	18	19	20
C	D	B	A	B	D	D	B	A	C

Section C

21. common 22. beggars 23. lying 24. poor 25. elderly

26. living 27. plastic 28. search 29. passers-by 30. vulnerable

31. media 32. comfortable 33. pretend 34. homeless 35. offer

36. cheated 37. miserable 38. finish 39. restaurant 40. pack

Part Three　Reading Comprehension

Section A

41	42	43	44	45	46	47	48	49	50
A	D	J	H	B	C	I	E	G	F

Section B

51	52	53	54	55	56	57	58	59	60
D	B	C	A	B	B	A	C	A	B

Part Four　Vocabulary

61	62	63	64	65	66	67	68	69	70
B	C	C	A	C	C	A	B	C	A
71	72	73	74	75	76	77	78	79	80
D	A	D	B	A	A	D	C	C	A

Part Five　Short Answer Questions

81. 8 years.

82. Improving the region's environment and infrastructure.

83. See Para. 2.

84. See Para. 3.

85. Western China Development strategy is the strategy carried out by Chinese government in 2000, which aims at accelerating the economic development and social progress and safeguarding and protecting the right to subsistence and development of the people in that part of the country.

Part Six　Translation

86. He is <u>keen on</u> all kinds of sports, especially on football.

87. The young people should try to <u>keep up</u> with the times.

88. The volcano erupts <u>once in a while</u>.

89. <u>In general</u>, diligent people tend to be successful more easily.

90. The government has taken some measures to <u>cope with</u> those tough social problems.

91. <u>No matter what</u> happens, I will always stand by you.

92. I was <u>at a loss</u> to understand his remarks on the forum.

93. The bearers of the voucher <u>are entitled to</u> get the discount in the shop.

94. You are so <u>considerate</u> that we really appreciate your arrangement for our trip.

95. He <u>claimed</u> that that medicine could cure the cancer.

Model Test 5

Part One Writing

What I have learned from My Mother

People always ask me all the time, 'How did you survive that?' or 'How do you do all this?' It's really because of my mother and the encouragement she gave me. She taught me how to face the difficulties in life.

As far as I remembered, my mom lived very simply. She was very strict with my older brother and me. She taught us how to be optimistic about the life. Life is always full of ups and downs. But my mother's philosophy is, 'If you get yourself in trouble, you've got to get yourself out of trouble.' When I was very young, my family was very poor, my mom always did what she can do to help father overcome the tough problems without complaining about how hard the time was. So the way my mother deals with thorny problems heavily influences me.

I know smooth life is never an easy road to take. But I have learned from my mother the secret of being brave in any and every situation, whether well fed or hungry, whether living in plenty or in want.

Part Two Listening Comprehension

Section A

1	2	3	4	5	6	7	8	9	10
B	C	A	C	D	D	B	A	B	A

Section B

11	12	13	14	15	16	17	18	19	20
D	C	B	A	C	D	A	B	C	A

Section C

21. Generation 22. difference   23. attitudes   24. especially   25. parents

26. know   27. environment   28. lifestyle   29. mind   30. ordering

31. wrong   32. present   33. develops   34. quickly   35. catch

36. trends   37. requirements   38. adjusted   39. particular   40. difficult

Part Three   Reading Comprehension

Section A

41	42	43	44	45	46	47	48	49	50
C	F	G	J	A	B	D	H	E	I

Section B

51	52	53	54	55	56	57	58	59	60
A	C	D	A	C	D	C	A	B	C

Part Four   Vocabulary

61	62	63	64	65	66	67	68	69	70
A	D	A	C	A	B	C	A	B	D
71	72	73	74	75	76	77	78	79	80
D	A	B	C	D	D	A	C	A	C

Part Five   Short Answer Questions

81. Foot binding was practiced in China for 1000 years. Young girls would have their feet wrapped, thus limiting the normal development and essentially crippling them.

82. About 3 years old.

83. The foot binding started in the 9th century when an Imperial concubine had her feet bound because her Prince loved her little feet. Other women started copying this practice.

84. In 1949.

85. It is difficult for them to buy suitable shoes for their small feet.

Part Six   Translation

86. My parents were out, so I could <u>have</u> the computer <u>to myself</u>.

87. He is much quicker than me to <u>catch on</u> to new knowledge.

88. You must be successful if you <u>set your mind to</u> one thing.

89. A number of problems <u>stand in our way</u> to success, so we have no choice but to solve one problem after the other.

90. Time is <u>running out</u>, let's finish it in three minutes.

91. He is the Top Five students in our class. <u>In addition</u>, he is also ready to help others.

92. No one can <u>hold back</u> the progress of the history.

93. When I entered the room, he glanced at me and <u>went on</u> reading the novel.

94. <u>Go ahead</u>, then turn right, you'll find the library.

95. We find it necessary to <u>help</u> those bankrupt companies <u>out</u> of the financial crisis.

Model Test 6

Part One Writing

Innovation is the Key to Success

Whether a nation or an individual makes progress or not largely depends on to what degree he or she is engaged in the innovation. This is what most of people draw the conclusion with the rapid development of society. So innovation becomes a key factor to achieve success.

First of all, the science and technology is developing at an astonishing speed. The speed is much higher than ever before. Only by keeping changing the old ideas do the people keep abreast of the times. Second, the economy now grows by leaps and bounds, any nation or company will be lagged behind without innovating their equipments and facilities, etc. Third, the people's living standard has improved dramatically in recent years. But a lot of people still cling to some outmoded beliefs, unwilling to abandon them. If they keep doing so, those people will become the old fogeys and as a result, their ideas and behaviors will be out of date sooner or later.

To sum up, to be innovative is essential to the development of any country or company, even an individual.

Part Two Listening Comprehension

Section A

1	2	3	4	5	6	7	8	9	10
D	A	C	D	A	B	C	A	B	D

156

Section B

11	12	13	14	15	16	17	18	19	20
B	C	A	D	B	B	A	B	C	A

Section C

21. temperature   22. common   23. industry   24. Celsius   25. Fahrenheit

26. inventors   27. former   28. astronomer   29. Germany   30. devised

31. scales   32. 1744   33. respectively   34. blank   35. marked

36. boiling   37. equal   38. melting   39. apart   40. claimed

Part Three   Reading Comprehension

Section A

41	42	43	44	45	46	47	48	49	50
D	J	A	I	G	C	B	H	F	E

Section B

51	52	53	54	55	56	57	58	59	60
D	B	C	B	A	D	B	A	C	A

Part Four   Vocabulary

61	62	63	64	65	66	67	68	69	70
A	C	B	C	A	A	C	A	B	C

71	72	73	74	75	76	77	78	79	80
D	A	C	A	C	B	C	A	C	D

Part Five   Short Answer Questions

81. Milan, Ohio; Port Huron, Michigan.

82. A newsboy, selling the newspaper and candy at the railway station.

83. In 1859.

84. The tin foil phonograph, On August 12, 1877.

85. For a successful person, hard work is the most important thing, and then his intelligence. So to achieve success, one must take great effort to do what he can do.

Part Six   Translation

86. The government has taken a number of measures to <u>bring down</u> the noise pollution in city center.

87. Since then on, he began to <u>be detached from</u> social and emotional involvement.

88. She <u>would rather</u> die than surrender to the enemy.

89. I watched him walked out of the room, until he was <u>out of sight</u>.

90. The minority groups are trying to <u>keep their cultures from</u> disappearing.

91. <u>Take it easy</u>, everything will be all right.

92. Catherine was so frightened that he had to <u>hold tight onto</u> herself to shriek.

93. I will <u>prescribe</u> some medicine for you, bear in mind that you take it three times a day.

94. He <u>slid</u> on the ice and fell down.

95. <u>Acid</u> rain erodes the soil greatly.

Model Test 7

Part One   Writing

My Attitude towards War

No sooner had the people mentioned the war than people argued each other heatedly. Some people think war is really a disaster to the human beings, while others are quite opposite. They think war is a way to balance the power among the countries in the world. In my opinion, I agree with the first group.

Human beings went through two world wars in the first half of the 20th century. In the short span of 30 years, millions of people died in the world wars, which left mankind with unprecedented destruction and carnage and thought-provoking lessons. After the world wars, people have realized that there are on winners in the war.

The reasons why some countries launched the war are as follows: firstly, they want to extend their territories so as to become a superpower. And secondly, the war some countries launched aimed at seizing as much natural resources as they could. Last but not the least, for some countries, starting a war was merely showing their national power, nothing else.

So, war is no good to each side, let's say no to war.

Part Two   Listening Comprehension

Section A

1	2	3	4	5	6	7	8	9	10
B	B	A	C	D	A	B	C	C	B

Section B

11	12	13	14	15	16	17	18	19	20
B	C	A	C	A	A	D	C	B	A

Section C

21. dramatic 22. Renaissance 23. Greek 24. theatre   25. combination 26. classical

27. changes 28. opera   29. form 30. German 31. influence   32. view

33. balance   34. important   35. aspects 36. traditional 37. entirely

38. emphasize 39. drama   40. called

Part Three   Reading Comprehension

Section A

41	42	43	44	45	46	47	48	49	50
C	H	F	A	G	B	I	D	J	E

Section B

51	52	53	54	55	56	57	58	59	60
A	C	A	C	D	D	B	A	C	A

Part Four Vocabulary

61	62	63	64	65	66	67	68	69	70
B	C	D	A	C	A	C	D	A	C

71	72	73	74	75	76	77	78	79	80
D	C	A	C	A	C	A	B	C	D

Part Five   Short Answer Questions

81. More than 55 million people.

82. The Treaty of Versailles and other peace agreements that followed World War I.

83. 1939, 1945.

84. Germany, Italy, and Japan.

85. The Treaty of Versailles and other peace agreements that followed World War I; the economic reasons; and The League of Nations fails to keep peach.

Part Six   Translation

86. The room is too small to <u>fit in</u> two more tables.

87. We went to the seaside last weekend and watched the sun <u>come up</u>.

88. After the match, we <u>headed for</u> the bar.

89. Women who <u>mean business</u> always do better than their male counterparts.

90. Work always <u>piles up</u> at the end of the month.

91. I was very tired this afternoon, but I really shouldn't <u>blow my top</u> like that.

92. My sister <u>took up</u> a job as a teacher three days ago.

93. Because of weather, we had to <u>call off</u> our trip.

94. I can <u>hold</u> his failure <u>against</u> him because he never tried for a passing grade.

95. She is unschooled <u>in the way of</u> the world.

Model Test 8

Part One   Writing

The Importance of Keeping Fit Mentally

Nowadays, with the standard of living improving, more and more people begin to concern about how to keep healthy not only physically, but also mentally. They do believe keeping mentally fit is of great importance.

Firstly, it is no denial that mental health does good to our work, study and life. It can enable us to deal with any problem we meet in an easy way. Otherwise, we will lose our heart after being confronted with setbacks. Secondly, mental health is also closely linked to physical health. They are interdependent. Keeping fit mentally exerts great influence on the physical health so that we can form a good habit of doing regular exercising, or balancing our diet.

All in all, keeping mentally healthy is an essential and necessary part of our life. It is very important to us all.

160

Part Two   Listening Comprehension

Section A

1	2	3	4	5	6	7	8	9	10
A	B	A	D	C	C	D	A	B	C

Section B

11	12	13	14	15	16	17	18	19	20
B	D	D	B	B	A	C	B	A	D

Section C

21. Austrian   22. 1856   23. founded   24. school   25. known

26. theories   27. developed 28. particular   29. patient   30. renowned

31. desire   32. energy   33. directed   34. objects   35. techniques

36. free   37. dreams   38. insight   39. passed   40. September

Part Three   Reading Comprehension

Section A

41	42	43	44	45	46	47	48	49	50
H	J	C	E	I	D	A	F	B	G

Section B

51	52	53	54	55	56	57	58	59	60
D	A	C	A	B	D	B	C	C	A

Part Four   Vocabulary

61	62	63	64	65	66	67	68	69	70
D	C	A	D	D	C	A	B	A	C
71	72	73	74	75	76	77	78	79	80
A	D	C	D	D	A	D	A	C	A

Part Five   Short Answer Questions

81. The father of modern American shipbuilding.

82. A cashier.

83. Because Henry John Kaiser's wife liked the color pink most.

84. The major health care issues facing the nation.

85. Henry Kaiser spent much of his later years in Honolulu and developed an obsession with perfecting its urban landscape.

Part Six   Translation

86. His debts have <u>amounted to</u> several million dollars, now he has no money to repay those debts.

87. No any country has right to <u>interfere with</u> other's internal affairs.

88. Waste gas from the car <u>contributes to</u> the global warming.

89. He found it hard to <u>get along with</u> his roommates.

90. <u>Due to</u> bad weather, the flight to Sydney had to be cancelled.

91. After he worked hard for many years, all his dreams <u>came true</u>.

92. She <u>went about</u> the chores as soon as she went back home.

93. As the saying goes, one takes the behavior of ones' company, that is to say, environment can influence, even <u>shape</u> one's character.

94. This picture should <u>trace</u> back to the 16th century.

95. Looking up the sky, we saw a hawk <u>soaring</u> in the sky.

Model Test 9

Part One   Writing

Say No to Terrorism

People are taken aback every time they hear the news that some innocent people were killed in a suicide bombing attack by terrorists groups. People all over the world bear a grudge against terrorists or terrorist activities which have brought disasters and damages to them. They think people all over the world should be united to combat terrorism.

Firstly, every country has the responsibility for fighting against terrorists in their own country. It can't be too necessary to take any action. Secondly, the United Nations should play an active role in combating terrorism. Since September 11, terrorist attack in America, the UN has called for the immediate action against global terrorism. Great achievement has been scored in this battle. So the UN will double its efforts to fight

162

against terrorist. Thirdly, all countries should be united as one to launch full-scale anti-terrorist campaign. Only by this can people in the world live a safe, comfortable life.

In summary, combating terrorism is the common target of human beings. Let's say no to terrorism.

Part Two Listening Comprehension

Section A

1	2	3	4	5	6	7	8	9	10
C	C	B	B	B	C	B	A	A	C

Section B

11	12	13	14	15	16	17	18	19	20
D	D	C	A	C	D	C	C	A	B

Section C

21. global   22. place   23. Europe   24. 1918   25. conflict

26. million   27. caused   28. damage   29. surrendered   30. November

31. Nations   32. fighting   33. peace   34. Germany   35. Russia

36. ending   37. Paris   38. sign   39. objected   40. negotiated

Part Three Reading Comprehension

Section A

41	42	43	44	45	46	47	48	49	50
J	D	F	B	I	G	C	E	A	H

Section B

51	52	53	54	55	56	57	58	59	60
A	C	A	B	C	A	D	D	B	C

Part Four Vocabulary

61	62	63	64	65	66	67	68	69	70
A	C	A	C	D	D	B	A	C	A
71	72	73	74	75	76	77	78	79	80
B	C	D	A	C	A	C	D	A	C

Part Five   Short Answer Questions

81. The Last Will of Adolf Hitler.

82. Martin Bormann.

83. The gallery in Hitler's home town of Linz on Donau.

84. 12 years.

85. Committing suicide.

Part Six   Translation

86. The man did a lot of wrong things. Suddenly, he <u>met his end</u> in his house at one night.

87. He was charged with murder and would be <u>strung up</u> in public.

88. When I was walking on the street, Jack waved his hand, <u>calling me in</u> his store.

89. They found that the burglars had <u>broken in</u> when they came back.

90. He fell ill as all the pressures <u>built up</u>.

91. In the <u>meantime</u>, he has picked up several foreign languages.

92. The deputy will be <u>in charge of</u> the work while the general manager is away.

93. When I'm free, I always <u>round up</u> several friends and play cards.

94. I hope that we'll <u>have done with</u> this work as soon as possible.

95. It has 4 years <u>to the day</u> since we met last time.

Model Test 10

Part One   Writing

The Benefits of Scientific Development

With the world moving toward globalization, the whole world becomes a small village in which people in every corner of the world can share their inventions and scientific achievements with their counterparts in other countries. The science and technology are developing at such a speed as is faster than ever before. Any breakthrough in science and technology takes less and less time to be put into practice. The scientific development has brought a lot benefits to human beings.

First, people's living standards improve greatly. The number of poor people or people living below poverty line is sharply reduced in recent years. More and more people have enjoyed a respectable standard of living. Second, better communication and transportation enable people to travel all over the world much easier. Third, the exchange between two countries becomes more and more frequent. People can learn each other's history and culture etc. so as to get acquainted with each other.

In conclusion, the development of science and technology not only brings the above-mentioned benefits to mankind, but also benefits people in different fields.

Part Two　Listening Comprehension

Section A

1	2	3	4	5	6	7	8	9	10
C	B	A	A	D	D	D	A	C	B

Section B

11	12	13	14	15	16	17	18	19	20
B	A	C	A	D	A	D	A	C	B

Section C

21. 1899　　22. actor　　23. famous　　24. director　　25. musician

26. Hollywood　27. considered　28. finest　　29. influenced　30. entertainment

31. 65　　　　32. stage　　33. performer　34. 88　　35. studio

36. character　37. manners　38. gentleman　39. tight　　40. bamboo

Part Three　Reading Comprehension

Section A

41	42	43	44	45	46	47	48	49	50
E	A	D	F	I	J	C	G	B	H

Section B

51	52	53	54	55	56	57	58	59	60
B	C	A	C	A	D	B	D	A	C

Part Four　Vocabulary

61	62	63	64	65	66	67	68	69	70
B	C	A	A	C	D	B	C	A	C
71	72	73	74	75	76	77	78	79	80
C	A	B	A	C	D	A	B	C	D

Part Five   Short Answer Questions

81. In 1543.

82. *On the Revolutions of the Heavenly Spheres*; *On the Fabric of the Human body*.

83. A foundation and origin of modern science.

84. That the intervening period saw a fundamental transformation in scientific ideas in physics, astronomy, and biology, in institutions supporting scientific investigation, and in the more widely held picture of the universe.

85. The period of scientific revolution.

Part Six

Translation: *Finish the sentences on Answer Sheet by translating into English.*

86. The story he told me yesterday <u>conjured up</u> the memories of my childhood in the countryside.

87. They spent many hours <u>laboring along</u> in the rain.

88. Things will get better as time <u>goes by</u>.

89. The cattle <u>feed on</u> the grass.

90. In the first lesson, the students are asked to <u>call out</u> their names in turn.

91. Nowadays, it takes less and less time to <u>put</u> new ideas <u>to work</u> in developed countries.

92. The money they saved for ten years is still <u>inadequate</u> for their round-the-world trip.

93. The film is condemned for <u>misleading</u> the audience.

94. In summer, remember to <u>apply</u> suntan lotion to your skin before you go out.

95. It is estimated that their annual earnings <u>average</u> $ 100,000.

Scripts for Listening

Model Test 1

Part Two　Listening Comprehension

Section A

1. **M**: Excuse me, could you tell me where I can find a bookstore?

   W: You can find one next to the supermarket across the street.

   Q: Where can the man find a bookstore?

2. **W**: What's wrong with you? You look so tired.

   M: I have got a fever and I feel so bad.

   W: You'd better see a doctor.

   M: Sure

   Q: What will the man probably do?

3. **M**: Could you help me send this greeting card to Jack?

   W: Of course, I'll do it right now. Can I send it by EMS?

   Q: What is the woman likely to do next?

4. **W**: What can I do for you?

   M: A cup of orange juice, a sandwich and a boiled egg. .

   Q: Where does the conversation probably take place?

5. **M**: What's wrong with your computer?

   W: It was broken. How can I do with it?

   M: You'd better have it fixed in the Computer Town.

   Q: What will the woman probably do?

6. **W**: Good morning, Mr. White, did you sleep well?

   M: Yes, the room is really comfortable. I'll check out at about 11 o'clock.

   Q: What is the probable relationship between the two speakers?

7. **M**: Tell me something about your trip to Sydney.

   W: I stayed there for two weeks. I ate a lot of seafood and visited many beautiful places. But I felt very tired after I came back.

Q: What is the woman talking about?

8. W: How much was your new jacket?

   M: It cost me 30 pounds, but I got it at half price.

   Q: How much is the regular price of the jacket?

9. W: There's a train every hour on the hour. What time is it?

   M: It's 9:50 am.

   Q: When will the next train arrive?

10. M: How do you feel today?

    W: I feel better now. But I still cough a little

    M: Follow my advice. Continue taking the medicine three times a day. Drink more water.

    Q: What is the relationship between the two speakers?

Section B

Passage One

In the UK, the grammar school is a school for the children over 11 years old who are academically smarter than others. It offers various kinds of subjects: English grammar and composition, Greek, mathematics, geography, etc. Later Latin was introduced as a volunteer class subject. It was said that William Shakespeare studied in the grammar school. But nowadays, there are few grammar schools in Britain. It is now considered outdated.

Questions 11 to 13 are based on the passage you have just heard.

11. What is the age limit of students who were admitted into the grammar school?

12. What are the subjects the grammar school offers EXCEPT _____?

13. What is the situation of grammar school now in Great Britain?

Passage Two

In 1908 the Olympic Games were first mentioned in a Chinese magazine. The Games of Los Angeles in 1984 were the first to have athletes from Taiwan as well as athletes from the PRC participating in the Olympics at the same time. The International Olympic Committee awarded the 2008 Olympic Games to Beijing on July13, 2001. The world has given Beijing a chance, and Beijing in turn will give the world a pleasant sur-

168

prise. In 2008, a perfect Olympic Games will be presented to the people of the world.

Questions 14 to 16 are based on the passage you have just heard.

14. When were the Olympic Games first mentioned in a Chinese magazine?

15. Where were the Olympic Games held in 1984?

16. When did China win the bid for the 2008 Olympic Games?

Passage Three

Thanksgiving Day is an important day in America. It is celebrated every year on the fourth Thursday of November. It has a very interesting history. Its origin can go back to the 17th century when the first thanksgiving dinner is said to have taken place. Some pilgrims from Europe came to America by the boat named "Mayflower" on December 11th, 1620. With the help of local Indians, they had a good harvest next autumn. In order to thank god, people began to gather together and ate different food, including turkey. This was the first Thanksgiving Day. Later turkey became a traditional food on that day. In modern days, people also eat pumpkin pies on Thanksgiving Day.

Questions 17 to 20 are based on the passage you just heard.

17. When is Thanksgiving Day today?

18. When did the first Thanksgiving Day take place?

19. Where did those pilgrims come from?

20. For whom did people thank in the first Thanksgiving Day?

Section C

The history of the English language is divided into three periods: The period from 450 to 1150 is known as the Old English. Old English grammar differs from Modern English grammar in many aspects.

The period from 1150 is known as the Middle English period. This period was marked by important changes in the English language. The change of this period had a great effect on both grammar and vocabulary. In the meantime, many Old English words were lost, but thousands of words borrowed from French and Latin appeared in the English vocabulary.

Modern English period extends from 1500 to the present day. The Early modern English period extends from 1500 to 1700. The nineteenth and twentieth centuries are a period of rapid expansion for the English vocabulary in the history of the English language.

Model Test 2

Part Two   Listening Comprehension

Section A

1. **M**: Good Morning, everyone!

   W: Good Morning, sir!

   M: Yesterday, we stopped at the page 7. Today I will give you a lecture on English grammar.

   Q: What does the man probably do?

2. **W**: When is the book due?

   M: You must return these books to the library by the end of July.

   Q: What is the probable relationship between the two speakers?

3. **M**: How was your journey by air?

   W: Very fine, it' very smooth.

   M: You must be very tired. This way, please, the car is waiting outside.

   Q: Where did the conversation probably take place?

4. **W**: What did you do last night?

   M: I did nothing but my homework.

   Q: What did the man do last night?

5. **M**: Hello, May I speak to Mr. Smith?

   W: Hello, sorry, Mr. Smith is having a meeting.

   M: When can I call him again?

   W: After 2:00 pm.

   Q: When will the man probably call Mr. Smith again?

6. **W**: Today it is my birthday. Would you like to attend my party tonight?

   M: I'm afraid not. I have got a lot of work to do at home.

   Q: Where will the man probably be tonight ?

7. **M**: How about bread and milk for the breakfast?

   W: Sounds very good, but I prefer boiled eggs.

   Q: What will the woman eat at breakfast?

8. **W**: How do you think about my blue jacket?

170

M: It's really terrific on you, really?

Q: What does the man think of the woman's jacket?

9. **W**: Would you like to change this 100-yuan note into 10 10-yuan notes?

M: Sure

Q: What is the man's probable job?

10. **M**: Mary, It's hot in the room, I wonder if you can open the door?

W: No problem.

Q: What will Mary do next probably?

Section B

Passage One

The American Civil War broke out in 1861 and ended in 1865. It was a war for abolishing the slavery in the South. And the four-year war began between the North and the South. The former wanted to abolish the slave system while the southern plantation owner tried their best to keep this system. The Civil War was a great disaster in American history. It brought great suffering to people in America, especially the southerners. Finally it ended in the victory of the Northern force.

Questions 11 to 13 are based on the passage you have just heard.

11. When did the American Civil War break out?

12. How long did the war last?

13. What was the result of the Civil War?

Passage Two

In America, there are two big parties: the Republic Party and the Democratic Party. The two Parties always compete with each other for the political power. Each party must choose their own candidate for the president. The candidate who wins the presidential election, will become the president of the USA, He will carry out the policies in the interest of the party he comes from. He will serve one term that lasts four years. If he succeeds in winning the next presidential election, he can serve anther term. But no president can serve more than two terms.

Questions 14 to 16 are based on the passage you have just heard.

14. How many parties are there in America now?

15. How long does a presidential term last?

16. How many terms can one American president serve at most?

Passage Three

Christmas is as an important festival for the Americans as the Spring Festival is for the Chinese. And it is also a festival for family reunion. It falls on December 25 every year. Originally, people honored and celebrated it for the birth of Christ. Nowadays, the first thing people usually do is to buy a Christmas tree and use it to decorate their houses. They put the color lights and pile the gifts on it. And then all family members gather around the tree, singing the Christmas songs.

On that day, people usually write down their wishes on the Christmas cards and send them to their friends. For the children, they are the happiest in the world on that day because they can't expect what kind of gift the Santa Clause will bring to them. For the adult, they can enjoy a one-week holiday so that they can share more quality time with their family.

Questions 17 to 20 are based on the passage you just heard.

17. When is the eve of Christmas?

18. What is the first thing people usually do for the coming of Christmas Day?

19. From whom do the children expect to get the gift?

20. How long will the people usually enjoy their Christmas holiday?

Section C

New York is located on the coast of the Northeastern United States at the mouth of the Hudson River. It has a population of more than 8 million, making it the largest city in America by population. It covers an area of 321 square miles.

New York City includes five boroughs: Manhattan, Brooklyn, Bronx, Queens and Richmond. The New York Metropolitan Area is mainly in Manhattan, it is the largest urban area of business, finance, entertainment, culture, fashion in America, even in the world. And UN headquarters is also situated in this area.

New York City is popularly known as, "Big Apple", and the "City That Never Sleeps," attracting people from all over the globe. By 2006, it is also known for its lowest crime rate among major cities in the U.S.

172

Model Test 3

Part Two   Listening Comprehension

Section A

1. **M**: Why are you late for the class?

   W: Sorry, there are so many cars on the street!

   Q: What is the reason for the woman being late?

2. **W**: Excuse me, sir, how many books can I take out?

   M: Five books at most.

   Q: Where does the conversation probably take place?

3. **M**: Hello Jackie, are you free tonight, would you like to go to the cinema with me?

   W: Sure, my pleasure.

   Q: What will the woman probably do tonight?

4. **W**: Where is my purse? I can't find it now.

   M: Don't worry. You must have left it at home.

   Q: Where is the woman's purse probably?

5. **M**: Nice to see the sun out again.

   W: True, but it's supposed to rain tomorrow.

   Q: What will the weather be like tomorrow?

6. **W**: I'm looking for a blue jacket, what would you recommend?

   M: We have the three sizes: big, medium and small. I think the second one is suitable for you.

   W: Ok, I'll take it

   Q: What size of jacket will the man buy probably?

7. **M**: After school, I will go to the supermarket, then have a supper in KFC, after that I will go to the cinema.

   W: I'd say you have a very busy day.

   Q: What will the man do immediately after school?

8. **W**: What will you do after graduation, to be a teacher or go on with your study?

   M: I have no idea.

   Q: What will the man do after graduation?

9. **W**: May I speak to Jack, please? This is Mary Speaking.

M: Sorry, Jack is out, would you like to leave a message?

W: Please let him call me back soon. Thank you.

Q: What will the woman do?

10. **M:** Will you go to that party Saturday evening?

　　W: If Mike goes there, I'll go too.

　　M: Mike said he will not go there.

　　Q: Will the woman go to that party?

Section B

Passage One

In 1994, UNESCO officially declared that the 5th of October is the World Teacher's Day. Since then on, almost 100 countries around the world celebrate World Teacher's Day on that day. It is to improve people's awareness of the contributions teachers have made and will make to the international education. It is also to call on people to show their respect to their teachers.

Teacher's Day will be celebrated at different dates in different countries. In India, people celebrate the Teacher's Day on the 5th of September. It was said that selection of the 5th of September as the Teacher's Day is related to one Indian President. He used to be a great teacher. On that day, it was his birthday. So Indian people celebrate the Teacher's Day on that Day. In China, the Teacher's Day falls on the 10th of September. On that day, Chinese students show their great respect and wishes to their teachers.

Questions 11 to 13 are based on the passage you have just heard.

11. According the UNESCO, when is the World Teacher's Day?

12. When is the Teacher's Day in India?

13. When is the Teacher's Day in China?

Passage Two

Teaching is one of the most honorable professions in the world. A teacher must have some qualities. The most important quality is profound knowledge, not only in the field of his own major, but also in different fields. Secondly, a teacher should be strict with his students both in class and after class. It is a must for a teacher. The third one is patience. A teacher ought to have much more patience than any other people, ready to answer any question the student may ask. Finally, a teacher should be a person full of pas-

174

sion and energy. All these qualities are very important for a good teacher.

Questions 14 to 16 are based on the passage you have just heard.

14. How many qualities for a teacher are mentioned in this passage?

15. Which is the most important quality a teacher should have?

16. Which is the last quality mentioned in the passage?

Passage Three

Harvard University is the oldest university in the United States. It was established in 1636. Harvard University was named after a young minister, John Harvard because he left his libraries and half of his estates to the university when he died in 1638. That was the beginning of the Harvard College. Now, Harvard University has become the most famous university in the USA, even all over the world. And seven American presidents graduated from this world-renown university. Harvard University includes Harvard College, Radcliffe College and 10 graduate and professional schools. Its law school, business school and medical college are among the best colleges in the world.

Questions 17 to 20 are based on the passage you just heard.

17. When was Harvard University established?

18. When did John Harvard die?

19. How many in US presidents graduated from Harvard University?

20. How many graduate schools are there in Harvard University?

Section C

American education system is quite different from Chinese education system. In most areas in America, the public education begins with the kindergarten classes for the five-year-old children. The children usually spend half a day attending classes in there. For the children from three to five, they may choose to go to the nursery schools or day care centers. That is pre-school education. When a child is about 6 years old, he or she will enter first grade. There are 12 grades for him or her to complete. The grade one to grade eight is called elementary school, and the grade nine to grade twelve is called high school. A high school graduate may go to college if his test scores are good enough to be admitted to one college or university.

Model Test 4

Part Two   Listening Comprehension

Section A

1. **M:** Hello, Holiday Inn, what can I do for you?

   W: I want to book a single-bed room this Saturday night.

   M: Sure.

   Q: What is the man?

2. **W:** Excuse me, is our food ready? We have sat there for about two hours.

   M: Please wait a minute, it'll be ready soon.

   Q: Where dose the conversation probably take place?

3. **M:** Yesterday I wanted to buy a book. But when I arrived there, the bookstore had already closed.

   W: Was it a holiday or a weekend?

   M: No, the bookstores close a bit earlier on Tuesdays

   Q: When did the conversation probably take place?

4. **W:** Hello, Jack, May I borrow your dictionary?

   M: Hello, Mary, sorry, Mike is using it at home now.

   Q: Where is the Jack's dictionary?

5. **M:** Paul is really a good engineer.

   W: Right, he has worked there since 2001 when he graduated.

   Q: When did Paul graduate?

6. **W:** Have you ever been to Hainan?

   M: Not yet, actually I want to go there, but I can't afford it.

   Q: What does the man mean?

7. **M:** Have you heard the news that the number of the new cars adds up to 300 in Beijing every day.

   W: Yes, I have also heard that there are 4 million cars in Beijing

   Q: How many cars are there in Beijing?

8. **W:** Good news, he will finish his book in May.

   M: Yes, I can't wait to read it.

   W: But I can't borrow the book in the library until July.

Q: When can the woman borrow the new book in the library?

9. **W:** How will you go to your hometown?

　M: I'll go there by train. But I used to go there by plane

　Q: How did the man go to his hometown before?

10. **M:** Look, it is raining now.

　W: Really, the school sports meeting will be held tomorrow, so it has to be put off until next week.

　Q: When will the sports meeting probably be held?

Section B

Passage One

As the human being enters the new century, poverty remains a global problem. According to the World Development Report 2000/2001, of the world's 6 billion people, 2.8 billion live on less than $2 a day and 1.2 billion on less than $1 a day. Eight out of every 100 infants do not live to see their fifth birthday. Nine of every 100 boys and 14 of every 100 girls who reach school age do not attend school.

Questions 11 to 13 are based on the passage you have just heard.

11. How many people are living on less than $2 a day in the world?

12. How many people are living on less than $1 a day in the world?

13. How many boys in their school age can't go to school per 100?

Passage Two

A lot of people in the world are facing hunger every day. About 25,000 people die every day of hunger or hunger-related causes, according to the United Nations. This is one person every three and a half seconds. Unfortunately, it is children who die most often. The main reason is lack of money. They can't have money to buy enough food. Being hungry for a long time makes them weaker and weaker. But in order to earn some money, they have to work, which then makes them even poorer and hungrier. The best way to help them escape from hunger is education.

Questions 14 to 16 are based on the passage you have just heard.

14. How many people will die of hunger or hunger-related causes everyday?

15. How many people will die of hunger in 7 seconds according to the passage?

16. Which of the following is the best way to lift people out of poverty?

Passage Three

India won its independence in 1945. Since then on, India's population increased rapidly and especially its population rose by 21.34 % between 1991 and 2001. Now it has a population of more than 1.1 billion, roughly one-sixth of the population. With a large population, India is also facing a severe poverty problem. More than one-fourth of the world's poor live in India.

Questions 17 to 20 are based on the passage you just heard.

17. When did India win its independence?

18. At what rate did India's population rise between 1991 and 2001?

19. How many people are there in India?

20. How many of world's poor people are living in India?

Section C

It is common to see beggars or the homeless lying on the ground begging for money in the big cites like Beijing, Shanghai etc. Some poor people, usually the elderly women in large cities make a living by collecting plastic drink bottles. Every day, they search for the drink bottles from one dust bin to another. Some of the passers-by may give out some money to those vulnerable people or the disabled. But recent reports from the media that some of the beggars are not real beggars, they either lead a comfortable life after "working hours", or pretend to be as poor as the homeless. So when people offer the help, they feel being cheated sometimes. But basically they are very miserable. If you don't finish the food in the restaurant, you may pack them up and give them to the poor, or the homeless you meet.

Model Test 5

Part Two   Listening Comprehension

Section A

1. **M:** Hello, it's Sunday today, but you look so busy.

   W: Yes, I'm preparing for my coming birthday party the day after tomorrow.

   Q: When is the woman's birthday?

178

2. **W:** How long do you usually go to school every day?

   M: It depends, 30 minutes by subway, 15 minutes by bus, and 10 minutes by taxi

   Q: Which is the slowest way for the man to go to school every day?

3. **M:** How did you do in the final exam?

   W: Not good, I failed in English and math.

   Q: How many subjects did the woman fail in?

4. **W:** I have prescribed something for you, make sure you'll take it twice a day.

   M: Sure, thanks a lot

   Q: What is the job of the woman?

5. **M:** Did you watch the soccer game yesterday?

   W: Nice game. The home team defeated the guest team by 5:0.

   Q: What was the result of the soccer game?

6. **W:** What time is it?

   M: It's 11:30 am, did Jack come back home?

   W: Sure, he came back two hours ago.

   Q: When did Jack come home?

7. **M:** Have you heard that Mike quit his job yesterday?

   W: For what reason? Underpaid? Or he didn't like it

   M: No, actually he was fired for his own mistake.

   Q: Why was Mike fired?

8. **W:** Your English is really good! You must have learned it for many years.

   M: Oh, I began to learn it fifteen years ago.

   Q: How many years did the man study English?

9. **M:** Did you get any gifts on Christmas Day?

   W: A lot of gifts, a teddy bear from my Day, a doll from my Mum, and a pen from John.

   M: Which one did you like best?

   W: The teddy bear.

   Q: Whose gift dose the woman like best?

10. **M:** Excuse me, Madame, please pull over.

    W: What's up?

    M: For your speeding.

    Q: What is the man's job?

Section B

Passage One

Mother's day is a day of celebrations for mums. It falls on the second Sunday in May. In the United States, Mother's Day was firstly celebrated in 1872. But until 1914, US president Woodrow Wilson officially announced that the second Sunday of May was the national Mother's Day. Since that year on, most states in America began to celebrate on that day. Nowadays, many countries all over the world celebrate Mother's day on that day.

Questions 11 to 13 are based on the passage you have just heard.

11. When is Mother's day?

12. When did the American people celebrate their first Mother's day?

13. When did Mother's Day become a national holiday in America?

Passage Two

The Mother's Day should be traced back to the ancient Greek. In spring, ancient Greeks held celebrations in honor of Rhea, the Mother of the Gods. Now many countries including the USA, Denmark, Finland, Italy, Turkey, Australia and Belgium celebrate Mother's Day on the Second Sunday in May. But other countries celebrate Mother's day in different days. For example, Mother's Day falls on December 8 in Spain and on the last Sunday of May in France.

Questions 14 to 16 are based on the passage you have just heard.

14. Where did Mother's Day originate?

15. Which season did Greek people celebrate a holiday for the Mother of the Gods?

16. When do the Spanish people celebrate their Mother's Day?

Passage Three

Children's Day is celebrated in many parts of the world. It is a day for children all over the world. Children will enjoy a day off on that day. In August 1925, some 54 representatives from different countries gathered together in Geneva, calling for the cooperation to protect the rights of children and prevent the child labor. Since that year on, many countries all over the world designated a day to celebrate Children's Day. But Children's Day is different in each country. Before the People's Republic was founded, the Children's Day was celebrated in the fourth of April since the first Children's Day was observed in 1932. But with the founding of new China, the Chinese government made an official announcement that June 1 was the International Children's Day on December 23, 1949. May 5 is Children's Day in Japan. It became a national holiday in 1948.

Questions 17 to 20 are based on the passage you just heard.

17. From which year did the first Children's Day begin to be celebrated in the world?

18. When was the first Children's Day celebrated in China?

19. When was the first Children's Day celebrated on June 1 in China?

20. When is the Children's Day in Japan?

Section C

Generation gap refers to a broad difference in values and attitudes between one generation and another, especially between young people and their parents. Why is there such a big gap between the children and parents? As we all know, the environment has changed, so has the lifestyle and that changes the mind of children. Today's generation doesn't like parents ordering them, and if they try and tell them what's wrong with them. And at present, the society develops very quickly and the parents can't catch up with new trends and requirements, because they have adjusted to a particular lifestyle. So they find it difficult to change it.

Model Test 6

Part Two   Listening Comprehension

Section A

1. **M:** Have you read the book about the war in that country?

   W: Yes, it was terrible. A quarter of million people died in the war.

   Q: How many people died in the war?

2. **W:** Excuse me, can you tell me how to get to the public library?

   M: Go straight along the street. Then turn left at the first stop light, continuing walking for a while, then you will find it very soon.

   Q: What should the woman do when she arrives at the first stop light?

3. **M:** Please help me dial the number 62040334?

   W: Wait a minute, sorry, it's a wrong one.

   M: Sorry, it should be 62040343.

Q: What is the right number the man wants to dial?

4. **W:** Where is my book I left on the desk yesterday?

   M: I gave it to your classmate, Jack.

   Q: Where is the woman's book?

5. **M:** Have you heard the announcement of the flight schedule?

   W: Sure, because of bad weather, plane to Beijing at 10:30 am will be delayed. It will take off an hour later.

   Q: When will the plane to Beijing probably leave?

6. **W:** Do you know Mike is learning English?

   M: Really, he used to learn civil engineering, then switched to finance.

   Q: What did Mike learn at first?

7. **M:** This is the best food I ever ate in this place.

   W: Well, let's order one more.

   Q: Where does the conversation probably take place?

8. **W:** Excuse me, can I meet Mr. Smith?

   M: Sorry, he will have a meeting from 2 p.m. to 3 p.m., and then he will meet a client.

   Q: What is Mr. Smith probably doing at 2:30 p.m.?

9. **M:** Have you got the ticket to tomorrow's concert?

   W: Not yet. I'm planning to buy it today.

   Q: When will the concert be held?

10. **W:** Hello, Jack, I heard that you are ill recently, Are you fine now?

    M: Hello, Mary, I think you must have mistaken me for my twin brother, Tom.

    Q: Who fell ill recently?

Section B
Passage One

Earnest Hemingway was born in Chicago on July 21, 1899. His father was a very wealthy doctor. He found a job as a reporter immediately after he finished the high school at the age of 18. Later he joined the army and went to the front in France. But then he went to Italy where he was seriously wounded. Returning home from the war, he began writing the novel, short stories, etc. Hemingway died on July 2, 1961.

Questions 11 to 13 are based on the passage you have just heard.

11. When was Hemingway born?

12. Where did Hemingway first go after joining the war?

13. When did Hemingway graduate from his high school?

Passage Two

Earnest Hemingway was a famous American novelist and short story teller. He wrote a number of novels and short stories. He finished his first book *Three Stories and Ten Poems*. in 1923. His most world-famous works are: *The Sun Also Rises*, *A Farewell to Arms*, *For Whom the Bell Tolls* and *The Old Man and the Sea*. For his novel and short stories, he was awarded a Noble Prize for Literature in 1954.

Questions 14 to 16 are based on the passage you have just heard.

14. When did Earnest Hemingway finish his first book?

15. Which of the following is NOT one of Hemingway's works?

16. When was Hemingway awarded the Nobel Prize?

Passage Three

The degree Celsius (°C) (摄氏) scale was devised by dividing the range of temperature between the freezing and boiling temperatures of pure water at standard conditions (sea level pressure) into 100 equal parts. Temperatures on this scale were at one time known as degrees centigrade, however it is no longer correct to use that term. The degree centigrade (°C) was officially renamed Celsius in 1948 to avoid confusion with the angular measure known as the centigrade.

Questions 17 to 20 are based on the passage you just heard.

17. What measure is the degree Celsius?

18. How many equal parts is the range of temperature divided into?

19. What is the original name of temperatures on the scale?

20. When did the official name of degree Celsius begin to be used?

Section C

Two temperature scales are in common use in science and industry. They are the degree Celsius (°C) scale, and the degree Fahrenheit (华氏温度). Celsius and Fahrenheit were both names of the inventors of two scales. The former was a Swedish astronomer and the latter came from Germany. Celsius and Fahrenheit devised their own temperature scales in 1744 and in 1724 respectively. Celsius took a blank thermometer, marked the boiling point of water and the melting point of ice and marked it off into 100 equal degrees. In Fahrenheit's scale the melting point of ice 32° and the boiling point of water 212° are 180 degrees apart. He also had a third point, the temperature of human's body which he claimed was 98°.

Model Test 7

Part Two   Listening Comprehension

Section A

1. **M:** What will you do this evening?

   W: I'll go to cinema, and then I'll have a dinner with my friends.

   Q: What will the woman probably do after the film?

2. **W:** Hi, Michael.

   M: Hi, Jane.

   W: Have you finished your paper?

   M: Not yet. We're required to hand in it next Tuesday.

   W: Neither have I.

   Q: How are the two speakers doing with their papers?

3. **M:** How many students are there in your class?

   W: There are 50 students, 40 girls and 10 boys.

   Q: How many girls are there in the woman's class?

4. **W:** Well, there are a lot of fruit.

   M: I like most of them, what about you?

   W: I like banana, pineapple and watermelon. But I like plum best.

   Q: What's the woman's favorite fruit?

5. **M:** Did you watch the soccer match yesterday?

   W: Yes, it's really a close game.

   M: What's the result?

   W: It's 3 to 2 in our favor.

   Q: How many goals did the speaker's home team score?

6. **W:** How did you do in your final exam?

   M: Oh, well, I feel really bad. I only answered the first three questions and I didn't finish the last two questions.

Q: Which of the following statements is TRUE according to the talk?

7. **M**: Long time, no see. How was your trip to Beijing?

   W: Wonderful. I visited a lot of places of interest.

   M: What are they?

   W: The Great Wall, the Summer Palace, Tiananmen Square, but the Forbidden City impressed me most.

   Q: Which place of interest did the woman like best?

8. **W**: Your shirt is very beautiful.

   M: Thanks, I bought it yesterday.

   W: How much is it?

   M: It is 20 dollars. But I got it at half price.

   Q: How much did the man pay for his shirt?

9. **M**: Do you remember your ID card number?

   W: Sure.

   M: Please tell me your last four numbers of your ID card?

   W: It's 1735.

   Q: What are the last 4 numbers of the Woman's ID card?

10. **W**: Your English is really good. Your major must be English.

    M: Yes, you are right. But I studied law first, then Chinese literature, finally I chose English as my major.

    Q: What did the man study at the beginning?

Section B

Passage One

Drama is the specific mode of fiction represented in performance. It comes from a Greek word meaning "action".

Dramas are performed in various media: theatre, radio, film, and television. Drama is often combined with music and dance: the drama in opera is sung throughout; musicals include spoken dialogue and songs; and some forms of drama have regular musical accompaniment. The most famous playwright in English literature is William Shakespeare, who wrote 37 plays in his whole life, including tragedies, comedies and historical plays.

Questions 11 to 13 are based on the passage you have just heard.

11. Which language does the word "drama" come from?

12. According to the passage, drama can be performed in the following media EXCEPT.

13. Which of the following can the drama be combined with?

Passage Two

Beijing opera or Peking opera is a form of traditional Chinese theatre which combines music, vocal performance, dance etc. It arose in the late 18th century and became fully developed and recognized by the mid-19th century. It is known as China's national opera and widely regarded as the highest expression of the Chinese culture. It is the most refined form of opera in the world and one of the three main theatrical systems in the world. Although it is called Peking Opera, its origins are not in Beijing but in the Chinese provinces of Anhui and Hubei. Now, it has also spread to other countries such as the United States and Japan.

Questions 14 to 16 are based on the passage you have just heard.

14. When did the Beijing opera rise?

15. When did Beijing opera fully develop?

16. Where did Peking opera originate?

Passage Three

Questions 17 to 20 are based on the passage you just heard.

The origin of the drama dates back to the ancient Greece. In early time, there are three types of drama in Greece. They were tragedy, comedy, and satire. The dramas were written as a part of the celebrations of the god, which were held once a year. Every year three authors were chosen to write three dramas, and one satire each. Similarly, five authors were also chosen to write three comedies and a satire play each. Each tragedy was then performed in 3 successive days, and on the last day the 5 comedies competed. But in modern people's eye, tragedy is a kind of drama with a sad or tragic ending. The comedy aims at amusing the audience. Satire is a literary work in which human vice or folly is attacked through irony, derision, or wit.

17. Where was the birthplace of drama?

18. How many types of drama were there in ancient Greece?

19. How often were the celebrations of the god held in ancient Greece?

20. What is a play with a tragic ending called?

186

Section C

Western opera is a dramatic art form, which arose during the Renaissance in an attempt to revive the classical Greek drama tradition. Both music and theatre were combined in the Greek Drama. Due to the combination with western classical music, great changes have taken place in opera in the past four hundred years and it is an important form of theatre until this day. The German 19th century composer Richard Wagner exerted enormous influence on the opera tradition. In his view, there was no proper balance between music and theatre in the operas of his time, because the music seemed to be more important than the dramatic aspects in these works. To restore the connection with the traditional Greek drama, he entirely renewed the operatic format, and to emphasize the equally importance of music and drama in these new works, he called them "music dramas".

Model Test 8

Part Two   Listening Comprehension

Section A

1. **M:** What's the weather like today?

   W: The forecast says it will rain in the morning, then it stops, but it is cloudy in the afternoon. Then it will rain again in the evening.

   Q: What is the weather like in the afternoon?

2. **W:** You look pretty in this pair of sunglasses.

   M: Really? It's a gift from my mum.

   W: I want one. Where can I buy them?

   M: My mum said they are only sold in Europe, not in China.

   Q: Where can the woman buy this kind of sunglasses?

3. **M:** Will you sign up for the course this term?

   W: I'm not sure. What's the schedule for the course?

   M: It begins at 2:00 pm and ends at 4:00 pm every Thursday.

   W: That sounds good.

   Q: How long does the course last every time?

4. **W:** Have you watched the film?

   M: Yes, I just finished it.

W: How did you feel about this movie?

M: It's boring at the beginning, but it has a surprising ending. On the whole, it's good.

Q: How did the man think about the beginning of the film?

5. **M:** Excuse me, what time is it?

W: It's 5:55. But my watch is five minutes fast.

Q: What time is it now?

6. **W:** Excuse me, can you tell me how to get to the post office?

M: Sure, go down this street, and then turn left at the first corner, go ahead, then you'll find it, it is next to the supermarket and KFC, opposite to the Bank.

Q: Where is the post office opposite to?

7. **M:** It's really amazing that you can speak four different languages.

W: That's true. Actually, I have learned English for 10 years and French 8 years.

M: Amazing. How long did you learn the other two languages?

W: Well, I began to learn Japanese 5 years ago and German, 4 years ago.

Q: Which language did the woman begin to learn 8 years ago?

8. **W:** Look, the bus is coming.

M: Great, it's ten minutes late due to the heavy traffic.

Q: Why is the bus late?

9. **M:** It's June, 2008. But the new building has not been completed.

W: Yes, It has been built for 2 years.

Q: When did the building begin to be built?

10. **W:** Congratulations! You have been admitted to MIT.

M: Thanks a lot. I've applied for the three-year graduate program.

Q: How long will the man study in the United States?

Section B

Passage One

Daydreaming was long held in bad reputation in society and was associated with laziness. In the late 1800s, Toni Nelson argued that some daydreams are self-satisfying attempts at "wish fulfillment". In the 1950s, some educational psychologists warned parents not to let their children daydream, for fear that the children may be sucked into "mental problems"

188

Questions 11 to 13 are based on the passage you have just heard.

11. According to the passage, what is the daydreaming closely related to?

12. When did Toni Nelson argue that some daydreams are self-satisfying attempts?

13. What did some psychologists warn the parents not to do in the 1950s?

Passage Two

In the late 1960s, psychologist Singer, from Yale University and psychologist Antrobus of the City College of New York created a daydream questionnaire. The questionnaire has been used to investigate daydreams. Psychologists Leonard Gambrels and George Huba used the questionnaire and found that daydreamers' imaginary images vary in three ways: how vivid or enjoyable the daydreams are, how many guilt-or fear-filled daydreams they have, and how "deeply" into the daydream people go.

Questions 14 to 16 are based on the passage you have just heard.

14. When was the questionnaire created by two psychologists?

15. Where did the psychologist Singer come from?

16. In how many ways did the daydreamers' images vary according to the passage?

Passage Three

Are daydreams good or bad? In 1974, a psychologist found three patterns in fantasy? two negative and one positive. Some people find that their daydreams are distracting. They have difficulty concentrating, their mind wanders, and their daydreams often make them anxious. A second pattern is represented by the person who has very negative daydreams filled with unpleasant emotions, guilt, self-torment, fears of failure, hostility, aggression and self-doubt. These people definitely do not enjoy their daydreams. Most people fall into the third pattern? The "happy daydreamer." They have pleasant daydreams and enjoy them, using them for self-amusement, future panning, problem solving and so on.

Questions 17 to 20 are based on the passage you just heard.

17. When did the psychologist find the three patterns in fantasy?

18. How many negative patterns did the psychologist find in fantasy?

19. Which of the following DOES NOT represent the second pattern?

20. Which of the following is what the "happy dreamer" has?

Section C

Sigmund Freud, an Austrian physician was born on May 6, 1856. He founded the school of psychology. Freud is best known for his theories of the unconscious mind. He developed his theory through a particular form of dialogue between a patient and a psychoanalyst. He is also renowned for his redefinition of sexual desire as the primary motivational energy of human life. It is directed toward a wide variety of objects, as well as his unique techniques, including the use of free association, and the interpretation of dreams as sources of insight into unconscious desires. He passed away on September 23, 1939.

Model Test 9

Part Two   Listening Comprehension

Section A

1. **M**: When will you come back tonight?

   W: I'm not quite sure. The movie will start at 5:00 pm and end at 7:25 pm. Then I will have a dinner with my friend.

   Q: How long does the film last?

2. **W**: This song is beautiful, but a little noisy. Whose song is it?

   M: I forget the singer's name. But I know all his songs are rock.

   Q: What kind of song are the two speakers' listening to?

3. **M**: Hello, Cindy, would you like to join our swimming club?

   W: Hello, Michael, I'm afraid not.

   M: Why?

   W: I can't swim. And I like playing soccer and basketball. So I'm afraid I have no time to swim.

   Q: Which of the following statement is NOT the reason why Cindy can't join the swimming club?

4. **W**: Look, I got a new mobile phone.

   M: It's terrific. It's Nokia N72.

   W: True, there are other types such as N71, N73 and N95.

   M: Really?

   W: But I prefer N95 to others.

   Q: What type of mobile phone did the woman get?

5. **M**: Have you heard that a strong quake hit that area?

190

W: Not yet. But I think it is a disaster.

M: Sure, it has claimed 2,000 people and injured 30,000.

Q: How many people have been killed in the earthquake?

6. W: How many words have your learned so far?

M: Oh, let's think. I have learned 2,000 words at college. But I learned 1,500 words at high school.

Q: How many words has the man learned?

7. M: Good morning, what can I do for you?

W: Good morning. I want to take a look at some apartments.

M: We have several kinds of apartments. The apartment with one bedroom, the one with two bedrooms, and the bigger one with three bedrooms.

W: Well, I want to look at the second kind.

Q: What kind of apartment is the woman probably interested in?

8. W: Why has the plane not come yet?

M: Don't worry. It was reported that the plane was delayed because of dense fog.

Q: Why is the flight late?

9. M: Madame, can I help you?

W: Yes, I want to order the dish, what's the special?

M: Well, we have spicy chicken, spicy beef and pork with peppers.

W: I prefer spicy chicken to the others.

Q: What does the women want to order?

10. W: How long does it take you to go to school every day?

M: It depends. It usually takes me 10 minutes to go there by bus, but 15 minutes on foot, and only 5 minutes by taxi.

Q: How long does it take the man to go to school by taxi?

Section B

Passage One

Adolf Hitler was born on April 20, 1889, in Austria. Adolf was very bright and talented when he studied at a village secondary school, but he felt uncomfortable in the much larger urban secondary school. He gave himself up to aimless reading, dreamed about becoming an artist, and developed a talent for evading responsibilities. Poor school marks prevented him from obtaining the customary graduation certificate. After the death of his father, he left for Vienna in 1907 to seek his fortune.

Questions 11 to 13 are based on the passage you have just heard.

11. When was Hitler born?

12. How were Adolf Hitler's school marks at secondary school?

13. When did Adolf Hitler move to Vienna?

Passage Two

In 1913, Hitler moved to Munich in the hope both of evading Austrian military service and of finding a better life in the Germany he admired so much. Opportunities were slimmer than that in Vienna. Hitler served throughout the war as a volunteer in a Bavarian infantry regiment. He was wounded in the leg in 1916. Significantly enough, he was never promoted to a leadership position, but he was awarded unusually high decorations for bravery in action. The war had a profound influence on him. He was especially impressed by, and learned much about, violence and its uses. Hitler the artist was dead, and the politician was soon to emerge.

Questions 14 to 16 are based on the passage you have just heard.

14. When did Hitler move to Munich?

15. Why did Hitler move to Munich?

16. When was Adolf Hitler wounded in the war?

Passage Three

It was generally accepted that cause of the death of Adolf Hitler on Monday, 30 April 1945 is suicide by gunshot and poisoning. The two methods that killed Hitler aroused people's suspicion that Adolf Hitler may have survived the end of World War II and people even showed their doubt what happened to his body. The records kept by the Russian KGB and FSB were released in 1993. And these records confirmed the widely accepted version of Hitler's death as described by Hugh Trevor-Roper in his book *The Last Days of Hitler* published in 1947. However, the Russian archives did show what happened to the Hitler's dead body.

Questions 17 to 20 are based on the passage you just heard.

17. When did Adolf Hitler die according to the passage?

18. How did Hitler kill himself?

19. Where were the records on Hitler's death kept?

20. What happened to Hitler's dead body?

Section C

World War I, also known as the First World War, the Great War, and The War to End All Wars, was a global war which took place primarily in Europe from 1914 to 1918. World War I was finally over in 1918. The first global conflict had claimed from 9 million to 13 million lives and caused unprecedented damage. Germany had formally surrendered on November 11, 1918, and all nations had agreed to stop fighting while the terms of peace were negotiated. On June 28, 1919, Germany and the Allied Nations, including Britain, France, Italy and Russia signed the Treaty of Versailles, formally ending the war. Versailles is a city in France, 10 miles outside of Paris. The United States did not sign the treaty, however, because it objected to its terms, specifically, the high price that Germany was to pay for its role as aggressor. Instead, the U.S. negotiated its own settlement with Germany in 1921.

Model Test 10

Part Two   Listening Comprehension

Section A

1. **M:** I bought the same MP3 player with yours. It cost me 200 Yuan.

   W: That's good. Mine is much more expensive. It was two times expensive than yours.

   Q: How much was the woman's MP3 player?

2. **W:** Where are you heading for?

   M: Well, I'm doing a research. I need some books. So I want to borrow some books.

   Q: Where will the man probably go?

3. **M:** What can I do for you?

   W: I'm looking for T-shirt.

   M: We have ablue one and a red one left. The blue one is of larger size. And the red, the small size.

   W: I want to red one.

   Q: What size of T-shirt does the woman want?

4. **W:** What are you reading now?

   M: I'm reading a novel of 160 pages.

   W: It's a thick one.

   M: Sure, but I have finished three-fourths of it.

   Q: How many pages of the novel has the man read?

5. **M:** Did you watch the NBA game last night?

   W: No. What was the result?

   M: It was 101 to 99. My favorite team was defeated.

   W: What a pity!

   Q: How many scores did the man's favorite team get in the game?

6. **W:** How did you do in the English-speaking contest?

   M: Not bad. The winner's score was only 1.2 higher than mine.

   W: Congratulations!

   Q: What prize did the man probably win in the English-speaking contest?

7. **M:** May I speak to Mr. Smith?

   W: Sorry, he's out.

   M: OK, may I call him back Wednesday morning?

   W: Wednesday morning, I'm afraid not. He will have a meeting. But Wednesday afternoon will be ok.

   Q: When will the man probably call Mr. Smith again?

8. **W:** Hello, Friendship Hotel. Can I help you?

   M: I want to book a room with a single bed on July 3.

   W: Wait a minute, let me check. Sorry. The room with a single bed is not available on that day.

   M: What kind of room do you have then?

   W: There is only one room with double bed left on July 4.

   M: Okay! I want this one.

   Q: What kind of room does the man finally book?

9. **M:** Hello, can I help you?

   W: Hello, would you like to change my 100-dollar note into five 10-dollar notes and one 50-dollar note?

   M: Certainly, wait a minute.

   Q: How many 10-dollar notes does the woman want to get?

10. **W:** I have learned that you're applying for studying abroad.

   M: Sure, I have sent my applications to seven universities all over the world.

   W: Did you get any offer?

   M: Only two.

   Q: How many universities have answered the man's application?

Section B

Passage One

The Industrial Revolution was a period in the late 18th and early 19th centuries when major changes in agriculture, manufacturing, and transportation had a profound effect on the economic and cultural conditions in Britain. The First Industrial Revolution, which began in the late eighteenth century, merged into the Second Industrial Revolution around 1850, when technological and economic progress gained momentum with the development of steam-powered ships, railways, and later in the nineteenth century with the internal combustion engine and electrical power generation.

Questions 11 to 13 are based on the passage you have just heard.

11. Where did the First Industrial Revolution break out?

12. When did the First Industrial Revolution happen?

13. Which of the following were NOT the achievements of the Second Industrial Revolution?

Passage Two

James Watt was born in Greenock on 19 January, 1736. Watt had little formal education due to poor health in his youth, but working in his father's shop he developed an interest in trying to repair things. Later he invented the most famous machine— steam engine, which was first used in pumping water. In 1882, 63 years after Watt's death, the British Association gave his name to the unit of electrical power and today James Watt's name is to be found written on almost every light bulb in the world.

Questions 14 to 16 are based on the passage you have just heard.

14. Why did James Watt receive little education in his youth?

15. What was James Watt most famous invention?

16. What unit is Watt's name used as today?

Passage Three

As the science and technology develops rapidly, the telephone has become a necessary part of our life. But who invented the telephone? As we all know, Alexander Graham Bell invented the telephone in 1876. The first words he spoke on his telephone were, "Watson, come here. I need you." Watson was his assistant's name.

That happened in 1875-76. However Antonio Meucci had a working telephone since 1848 in Havana and a perfected model by 1871. On that year Meucci filed for and obtained a patent for the telephone. To say that Bell invented the telephone is erroneous. Meucci invented it. The unfortunate thing about Meucci is that he did not renew the application for patent due to lack of money. Had he renewed it, Bell would not have been granted a patent. Bell knowing the facts applied and was granted a patent. Bell is not the inventor. He simply commercialized what had been invented by Meucci and made a fortune whereas Meucci died poor and destitute.

Questions 17 to 20 are based on the passage you just heard.

17. When did Alexander Bell invent the telephone?

18. Who really invented the telephone?

19. When did Antonio Meucci begin inventing the telephone?

20. Why didn't Antonio Meucci get the patent for his invention ?

Section C

Sir Charles Spencer Chaplin, was born on 16 April, 1889, better known as Charlie Chaplin, was an Academy Award-winning English comedic actor. Chaplin became one of the most famous actors as well as a notable director, composer and musician in the early to mid Hollywood cinema era. He is considered to have been one of the finest mimes and clowns, ever caught on film and has greatly influenced performers in this field. His working life in entertainment spanned over 65 years, from the Victorian stage and music hall in the United Kingdom as a child performer almost until his death at the age of 88. Chaplin is also one of the co-founders of United Artists, the movie studio that revolutionized Hollywood.

Chaplin's principal character was "The Tramp". "The Tramp" is a vagrant with the refined manners and dignity of a gentleman. The character wears a tight coat, oversized trousers and shoes, and a derby; carries a bamboo cane; and has a signature toothbrush moustache.